The Secret of the Missing Grave

The Secret of the Missing Grave

By

David A. Crossman

DOWN EAST BOOKS
Camden / Maine

ISBN 0-89272-456-0 (hardcover)
ISBN 0-89272-470-6 (paperback)

Printed at Sheridan Books, Inc.

2 4 6 8 9 7 5 3 1

Down East Books
P.O. Box 679
Camden, ME 04843
BOOK ORDERS: 1-800-685-7962

Library of Congress Cataloging-in-Publication Data

Crossman, D. A. (David A.)
The secret of the missing grave / by David A. Crossman.
p. cm.
Summary: Summering on a Maine island, thirteen-year-old Ab joins her friend Bean in investigating the odd noises in her boarding house and solving the mystery of a missing treasure and stolen paintings.
ISBN 0-89272-456-0
ISBN 0-89272-470-6 (pbk.)
[1. Islands Fiction. 2. Maine Fiction. 3. Mystery and detective stories.] I. Title.
PZ7.C882845 Sg 1999
[Fic]—dc21 99-21629
CIP

Dedicated to my son and daughter,
my nieces and nephews,
and the Bean and Ab in all of us.
Also to Rebecca Libby who looks just like Ab.

Contents

1

Ghosts in the Walls

"The Moses Webster House is haunted," said Ab. She skipped a stone in the direction of a little squadron of ducks that paddled along undisturbed in the cove. They seemed to sense they had nothing to fear. Abby wasn't very good at skipping stones, though she practiced every summer under Bean's expert tutelage.

"Everybody knows that," said Bean matter-of-factly. "You gotta get lower down, like this," he added, folding himself at right angles to the earth, "then heave, like this."

Ab pretended not to watch as the tiny, round-bottomed stone danced across the glassy surface as though it were winged and weightless. The ducks still didn't fly—she knew they wouldn't leave their little ones—but they sure scattered in a hurry. The first skips seemed miles apart. The rest got closer as the stone lost its momentum, then finally trickled into a little chatter of numberless splashes. She lost count at twenty-two.

"More wrist, less arm," Bean instructed. "Like I told you."

"Who cares?" said Ab. She flipped a wisp of red hair from her face.

"You look weird when you do that," said Bean.

Ab sank to her knees on the damp vegetation at the water's edge. She picked up a stick and poked at an empty urchin shell that had probably been a gull's dinner not long before. "Do what?" she said.

Bean kicked at a nearby chunk of granite and focused his impassive eyes on nothing in particular. "I don't know," he said enigmatically.

Ab was a girl this summer; that was the problem. Of course, she'd always been a girl, but he'd always been able to overlook it before. This summer, though, well . . . there wasn't any way around it. When she left last year, she was just Ab. Now she was thirteen and a girl all over the place. He'd noticed as soon as she got off the boat. When she did things like flipping her hair and tilting her head in that curious way, it just made it worse. That's what he was thinking, but he couldn't find the words to make sense of it, and he wouldn't have said them if he could.

Ab looked at him slyly and flipped her hair intentionally. She knew. She wasn't sure what exactly, but somewhere inside she knew.

Bean figured it was going to be a long, difficult summer. Already he was halfway wishing it was Labor Day and Ab and her folks were heading back to New York. He feigned an uninterested glance in her general direction.

Halfway wishing.

"You know about a ghost in that house?"

"Sure," said Bean. He sat down on a piece of sun-bleached driftwood. "I had a friend who lived up there before the Proverbs turned it into a B and B."

"You mean Dave Johnson?" said Ab. Her memory of the island and its inhabitants went back just as far as Bean's.

"Yeah," Bean replied, a little miffed at having lost the exclusive option on that piece of information. Fact was, most of the things worth remembering in his life involved Ab in one way or another. He knew that when she left in the fall, he'd get that feeling like a punctured balloon, same as always. Then the leaves would fall, and snow would cover the island like frosting on a frozen cake. He'd go to school, go skating and sliding, play basketball and baseball, work and have fun like everyone else, but he'd be only half there. The rest would be tucked up inside somewhere, warming its toes beside that little crust of summer in his heart, waiting for Ab to return.

"Well?" said Ab, a little impatiently.

"Well, what?" said Bean, quickly looking up and away.

"What did he say, Davey Johnson? Did he see the ghost?"

"Nope," Bean replied flatly. He let the word just hang there. He knew that would get her all worked up, and he didn't much mind if it did. After all, she was getting him worked up, whether she knew it or not.

"But . . . ," Ab said at last. "Come on, out with it."

"He used to say he heard things."

"What kind of things?"

Bean picked a piece of grass and stuck it between his teeth. "I'm not sure I should say."

"Why not?" Ab demanded indignantly.

"'Cause."

"'Cause why?"

"Well," said Bean, "you're stayin' there, ain't you? All summer long. I'd hate to scare you off."

"Don't you worry about me, Beanbag," said Ab, using his full nickname. "I'm not scared of anything."

"Didn't say you was, did I?" said Bean calmly. He drew the grass between his thumb and forefinger and let the seeds fall on the breeze. "You're the one who brought it up."

"So, what did he hear?" asked Ab, a little less belligerently. She wasn't sure she wanted to know any more about it, but she wasn't going to let him know that.

Bean lowered his voice confidentially. "Breathing."

"Breathing?" echoed Ab, wide eyed in spite of herself. "What kind of breathing?"

"Like this," said Bean. Leaning close to Ab's ear, he drew in a slow, mournful breath and squeezed it raspingly out to the tail end.

A splendid shiver trickled like ice down Ab's spine, and the fine golden hairs on her arms stood at attention.

Bean nodded. "And," he said mysteriously, "something else."

Ab's eyes popped open even wider. "What?"

"Footsteps."

"That's what I heard," cried Ab, unable to contain herself any longer. She jumped to her feet. "Breathing and footsteps."

"You did?" said Bean, nearly choking on his Adam's apple. He'd only been kidding.

"Yes. When I was in bed last night."

"What time was it?"

"I don't know. I went up about nine-thirty or ten, read a little while, then turned out the light."

Nothing remained of Bean's pretense. "What happened?"

"Well," said Ab, sinking once more to her knees and drawing Bean with her. She bent close to him. "At first I thought it was just somebody bumping around in the room upstairs," she said in a conspiratorial whisper.

"So? Maybe it was," Bean reasoned.

Ab shook her head dramatically. "Then I remembered there is no room upstairs, only attic."

This time when she flicked the hair from her face, Bean didn't even notice. "Really?" he said breathlessly.

She nodded.

"What'd you do?"

"Very, very slowly," said Ab, slipping easily into her storytelling mode, "I got out of bed and tiptoed to the door."

"Did you turn on a light?"

"No," Ab replied a little sharply. She hated to be interrupted just as she was getting started.

Bean was incredulous. He'd have turned on the light. Especially in that big, drafty old house. "I bet you did."

"Did not," Ab protested.

Bean let it pass. "Then what?"

"I opened the door, real quietly," Ab mimed the action in the air, "and went down the hall."

"Why down the hall?" said Bean impatiently.

"That's where the door to the attic is. Do you mind if I finish my story?"

"I wish you would," Bean retorted. "Just quit leavin' out stuff."

Ab rolled her eyes. "Anyway," she resumed with a touch of long-suffering, "I got to the door and pressed my ear against it. Thump! Bump! Bump!" She issued the sound effects suddenly and sharply so that Bean jumped in his skin.

"They're not footsteps," he said, dressing his discomfiture in indignation.

"The footsteps came next," Ab continued, pleased with the effect her narrative was producing. If she had to live with ghosts, Bean was sure by golly going to know what it felt like. She stamped on the ground. "But they weren't coming from the attic."

"Where, then?"

"I couldn't make that out," said Ab, lowering her voice further still. "One second they seemed to be coming from the walls, then the ceiling. Every time I thought I'd figured it out, they'd come from somewhere else."

"Wow," said Bean unwittingly. He hadn't meant to sound impressed.

"It was as if I was surrounded by ghosts in heavy shoes."

Bean was bug eyed. He didn't talk for a minute. He was too busy digesting what he'd just heard. "How long did the sounds last?" he said finally.

Ab shrugged. "I don't know. A minute, maybe. I was just going to go call my dad when they stopped."

For a while Bean pondered in silence. There had to be a rational explanation. That's what his mother would say. "I bet somebody was just putting luggage away or something," he declared.

"Who?" said Ab. "There are only six other people in the house, including the Proverbs, and they were all down in the kitchen playing cards. I heard them."

"Mice, then."

"Mice? I don't think so. Elephants maybe."

"What did they sound like?"

"What do you mean?" said Ab. "They sounded like footsteps."

"No. I mean, were they walking back and forth, around in circles, jumping up and down . . . ?"

"Oh, I see what you mean. Let me think." She forced her memory. "I think . . . yes, there was a kind of pattern. Up and down."

"Up and down?"

"Yeah. From the bottom of the wall to the top of the wall."

"Dash away, dash away, dash away all," said Bean automatically.

"Earth to Bean," said Ab, tapping him on the head.

He ignored her. "Did it sound like more than one person?"

"Or whatever," said Ab.

Bean allowed for that. "Or whatever. Was there more than one, do you think?"

Ab pondered again. "No," she said seriously. "I don't think so. Come to think of it, they weren't like footsteps at all, really."

"Oh, great."

"No," said Ab. "I mean, now that I think about it, they were more like . . . they weren't as regular as footsteps."

"More random, you mean?" Bean asked.

"Yeah, random," said Ab, a little surprised. "That's what I was going to say, but I didn't think you'd know what it meant." Actually, she hadn't thought of it at all, but it's the word she would have used, if she had thought of it.

"Thanks a lot."

"And something else," Ab recalled suddenly. "There was a kind of metal sound to them."

"Metal?"

"Yeah. It wasn't just thud, thud, like this," she said, stamping her foot on the ground. "It was more as if someone was dragging around one of those big, old cast-iron frying pans Mrs. Proverb has down in the kitchen. They weigh a ton."

Bean smiled slyly. "Strong mice."

"Elephants," said Ab, and they laughed.

"Then I heard the breathing."

Bean nearly swallowed his tongue. "You did?"

Abby looked at her watch. "Ice cream time."

They got cones from the little take-out on Main Street. Then they went to the wharf, where they made seats of some wire mesh lobster traps that someone had hauled out for repair. Bean had chocolate ice cream, as always. Ab had cookies 'n' cream, as always.

"That doesn't sound like any ghost I ever heard of," said Bean. He wiped his mouth on the sleeve of his T-shirt.

Ab was inclined to agree. "Well, whatever it is," she said, "it's real. I wasn't dreaming, and don't tell me it was my imagination."

"I won't," said Bean. "You don't have any imagination."

"Yes, I do!"

Bean shook his head. "Remember that day last summer when we spent an hour out on Lane's Island playing Creatures in the Clouds?"

Ab tossed the soggy end of her cone to the gulls and wiped her fingers furiously on the remains of her napkin. That was one of the things that bugged her about Bean: When he looked at clouds, he saw dungeons and battles, fiery chariots, and swirling sultans on flying carpets. All she saw, if she tried really hard, were puppies and kittens. What made it doubly bothersome was that he couldn't seem to concoct a decent ghost from all the ammunition she'd given him.

"I do have an imagination," she said in self-defense. "It's just a normal imagination, not a demented one like yours." She stuffed her dirty napkin down his neck and, with a squeal of laughter, dodged out of his reach as he took a swipe at her.

By the time Bean extracted the damp, sticky wad from beneath his shirt, Ab was halfway up the sidewalk leading to the Moses Webster House. Bean followed, but at the fountain he splashed water on his back and washed his hands. "I'll get you for that," he bellowed.

Ab had stopped in the front yard at the wood bench by the big forsythia and was staring at the house. The tower window seemed on fire with the golden rays of the setting sun.

"That was mean," said Bean, trotting up beside her. "Just wait. One of these days when you least expect it . . ."

Ab was only partly listening. She seemed miles away, lost in thought. "There's probably a good explanation," she said, more to herself than to him.

"Sure there is," Bean agreed quietly, so as not to intrude too sharply on her thoughts.

At that instant both of them caught a subtle motion in the tower window of the Winthrop House next door. A curtain had moved and a face appeared, watching. Neither of them could make it out, but they knew who it was. Abby shuddered visibly. "She gives me the creeps."

"That's strange," said Bean. "I've never seen her in the daylight before. I guess she's not a vampire after all."

2

The Treasure Tunnel

THAT NIGHT AB READ AWHILE IN BED, then lay in the dark listening so hard she could almost feel her ears pulsing. Nothing. A squirrel scurried across the floor above—they often found their way into old houses—and she heard the soft, comforting conversation of her parents as they got ready for bed. She heard the heavy drops of dew that the night collected from the fog as they fell from leaf to leaf in the trees, and she heard the distant foghorn on Puffin Ledge moan its weary warning to the dark. But of ghosts or eerie footsteps or things that go bump in the night, she heard not a whisper—until she was just beginning to drop into sleep.

So clear it made her sit bolt upright in bed, she heard it. Breathing. Deep, sonorous, and sad. And near. She could feel a chill, damp breath on the back of her neck. Behaving as any sensible girl would, she screamed at the top her lungs and dove under the covers.

Reinforcements were not long in coming. Scarcely had the echo of her cry died in the remotest corners of the house when a veritable herd of adults thundered down the narrow hall to her room.

Her father was first through the door. "Ab, what is it? What on earth happened?"

"Abby, are you all right?" said her mother, tossing herself on the bed and cradling Abby's head on her breast. "My poor baby. Did you have a nightmare?"

Suddenly Ab wasn't afraid anymore. Instead she felt embarrassed and a little silly.

"What was it, Tom? Is she okay?" said Mr. Proverb, who was now silhouetted in the doorway, tying his robe around himself.

Mrs. Proverb was right behind him. "If that scream didn't wake the dead, they'll sleep 'til Judgment."

"Oh, great," said Abby under her breath as the parade of adults continued to pour into her room.

Meanwhile, her mother felt her forehead to see if she had a fever, the same way she had when she was a child. Ab didn't really object. There was something comforting about it. Of course, she'd never say so.

Ab cast a sheepish glance at Mr. and Mrs. Proverb, who, seeing that she was all right, departed with a sleepy "good-night."

"What is it, Punkin'?" asked her dad softly.

Good question, thought Ab. "I thought I heard a noise," she said.

"What kind of noise?"

Ab squirmed a little. She knew that if she told them, they'd say, Oh, that's only the wind, or probably just the house settling. Still, they'd asked—and she had gotten them out of bed—so she told them.

"Breathing?" said her mother when she'd finished.

"Breathing?" her father echoed. "You mean like this?" He panted rapidly in and out, like an overheated Saint Bernard. Ab giggled.

"No," she said. "Not like that."

"It was probably just the wind," said her mother, patting her on the shoulder. Ab peeked out the window. The willow tree, which swayed in the slightest breeze, was perfectly motionless against the glow of the streetlight.

"Or the house settling," said her father reassuringly. It was as if they'd rehearsed their parts. He lowered her head to the pillow and tucked the covers up under her chin. "The only thing you've got to be afraid of is what's up here." He tapped her on the forehead. "You've got too much imagination."

Not to hear Bean tell it, she thought.

They left the room quietly and closed the door.

Abby was beginning to wonder if they were right. Maybe she had been imagining things. She'd nearly convinced herself of that and was just drifting off to sleep when the slow, metallic thumping began again. It was coming from her closet.

She modified her response this time. She didn't scream, but she did hide under the covers. It didn't help; the bumping sound continued. Surely her folks would hear it and come running to her rescue. They didn't.

Then, as quickly as it started, it stopped. Ab peeked out from under the covers and stared holes into the deep shadows in the corner of the room where the closet door stood partially open. For a long time she waited, the blood throbbing in her ears as she held her breath.

But someone else *was* breathing. Once again a long, low inward breath, carrying with it a sorrowful sigh, drew a faint rush of air by her ears. Then all was quiet.

"It's the house," said Ab as she and Bean ambled down the narrow path to the quarry. The sweet grass slapped at their ankles. Now and then, they spied a wild strawberry and stopped to pick it.

"Well," Bean replied, "you said it was haunted."

"No," Ab replied thoughtfully. "Well, yes—but I don't feel that it's something in the house. I mean, it's the house itself. As if it's alive."

Bean, holding an alder branch aside so Ab could pass, made eerie sound effects.

"What if it *is* alive?" Ab retorted emphatically. "Haven't you ever felt that a house has a soul, or something?" Bean rolled his eyes. "No, think about it. Sometimes, when you're sitting in a house, don't you feel as if you're being watched, even when there's nobody's home?"

"Nobody's home," echoed Bean. "You got that right." He tapped his temple.

Ab pressed on. "Haven't you ever had that feeling?" She stopped short and put her hands on her hips, as if challenging him to deny it. She knew her Bean.

"I suppose," Bean admitted grudgingly. "In an old house."

"Well, you sure would have that feeling at the Moses Webster House."

True, thought Bean. He would. The Moses Webster House was the biggest on the island. It had a tower in which a solitary window seemed to cast a stern eye over the town that Moses Webster had created. For a number of years, the house had stood empty, slowly falling into disrepair and inviting squirrels, bats, and homeless ghosts through its broken windows. Ever since the Johnsons had moved in and fixed up the place, Bean never looked at the house or thought of it without imagining it as it had been during those lonely, vacant years. The long fingers of the big dead elm tree in the corner of the front yard seemed to point at the tower on moonlit nights as if to say, best ye take the long way home than pass ye too close by.

Passersby automatically crossed to the far side of the road, and even the most hardened skeptic couldn't help but entertain the notion that, if ghosts did exist, the Moses Webster House would be the perfect place for them.

Bean shuddered.

"I think it's sad," said Ab, who had been talking all the while, but Bean hadn't heard her because he'd been wrapped up in his own thoughts.

"What's sad?" he said.

"The house," Ab replied as they arrived at the quarry. "Haven't you been listening to me?"

"Sure I have," he asserted in self-defense. Then his conscience caught up with him. "Well," he added, "I was thinking." He took off his T-shirt, blue jeans, and shoes, revealing baggy blue and yellow swim trunks from which he seemed to sprout like an undernourished scarecrow. His legs were blindingly white.

"Wow, we'll have to call you Frosty," she said, shielding her eyes mockingly.

She undressed to her new pink bathing suit. "What were you thinking about that was so important you couldn't listen to me?"

Casting a kind of sideways glance at Ab, Bean suddenly felt even more uncomfortable. "About whatever it was you said," he answered. "Last one in's a rotten egg." So saying, he hurled himself off the granite cliff at the cold green water below.

A year ago Ab would have been right behind him. Now, though, she merely sauntered casually to the edge and sat down, dangling her legs and waiting for Bean's copper-spangled head to bob out of the water. She knew it would eventually, out near the middle of the quarry.

On the surface Bean thrashed around as if he were about to drown, but underwater he was like a fish. He could swim much farther than anyone else, even the older teenagers, who were now sunning themselves on the rough-cut granite slag heap that towered over the other side of the quarry. Even they were impressed, and they threw pebbles to mark the spot where they thought Bean would surface.

This time, though, Bean came straight through his own cloud of bubbles and looked up the smooth-sided cliff at Ab, silhouetted thirty-five feet above against the bright blue sky. "You're a rotten egg," he proclaimed loudly, his voice echoing off the cliffs.

Ab pretended to brush something from her knee as she studied him down the length of her nose. "Don't be so childish," she said, sighing. Of course, things would have been different had she been able to beat him into the water.

Nevertheless, Abby's aloof attitude confused Bean more than ever, and somehow her words hurt him. "Oh, yeah?" he said, buying time for something clever to come to mind. "Well, what about putting that napkin down my back?" He was paddling awkwardly to keep his skinny body afloat.

Ab laughed lightly and tossed her head. "That was entirely different," she announced, as if it were. Which it wasn't.

"What about a house that's alive?" Bean retorted in his most annoying voice. Flailing away, he swam toward the ledges. Then he pulled himself out and began the long climb—by soggy little handholds and narrow, pebbly ledges—up the familiar cliffs. He was too angry to even notice how cold it was in those pockets of shadow.

Now why did I say that? thought Abby. It was as if something had suddenly come over her. She didn't think Bean was childish. She thought he was great. He'd been her best friend since the first summer she came to the island when she was four, and they'd shared a hundred wonderful adventures together.

The summer she was laid up with a broken leg, it was Bean who spent time with her, playing board games and reading books, when she knew he'd rather be out in his boat poking around the shallows. She remembered the times they tramped over Armburst Hill, with its craggy caves and spruce-covered granite ledges that rose high over the village. And the Trolly Pond cliff and its heart-stopping view of all Penobscot Bay. And to the south, Matinicus and Criehaven, those strange islands that some days seemed to float high above the horizon and other days—even perfectly clear days—couldn't be seen at all. To the west were the White Islands—spiked nests of evergreen against the backdrop of the rolling blue Camden Hills. Up the bay were North Haven, Islesboro, and Eagle Island and, to the north, Blue Hill and Mount Desert.

Ab took a deep breath. She might live in New York City, but her home was Penobscot Island. It always would be. "Good ol' Bean," she said aloud, just above a whisper. What had come over her anyway?

"I was just teasing," she apologized as Bean's red head poked above the ledge. "You're right. I'm a rotten egg."

Bean had been seething as he climbed. He'd been rehearsing what Ab would say, then imagining what he would reply. In fact, he had the whole conversation mapped out in his head, and it wasn't a very pleasant conversation, at that.

Now this.

There was only one thing for him to say. "I didn't mean that about the house being alive, either."

Ab smiled. "Well, I admit that it sounds pretty silly in the daylight. But at night . . ."

"I know. Things are different in the dark."

For a while they forgot about the strange noises. Instead they climbed down to the water and played and splashed and swam and dived in the little corner of the quarry they'd staked out for themselves.

When Bean went to chase a small trout into the emerald depths, Ab sat on a ledge with her legs in the water up to her knees. New York seemed a million miles away. There, all her friends were wearing makeup. Some had started to smoke. Some were dating. Some . . . well, as her dad said, they were thirteen going on thirty, and he didn't mean it as a compliment.

What would they think if they saw her here, hanging around with Bean? She could almost hear the mocking laughter. What would they think of Bean? They'd be hysterical.

Just then Bean's head broke the surface in a shower of spray made golden by the sunshine. He gasped and sputtered and made one of his silly faces. She smiled, but there was a trace of sadness to the smile. Those girls would never understand.

Too bad for them.

The sky was an unbelievable blue filled with puffy white clouds. They seemed to drift aimlessly around the heavens as they watched the deep magic of a Maine summer cast its spell on those fortunate enough to share it.

There were a lot of people in the quarry. Little ones in the slippery shallows just off the path shouted, "Look, ma. Watch. Ma!" while their mothers tried to carry on conversations with friends whose own children chirped the same timeless refrain. Boisterous teenagers stretched out on the granite slabs overhanging the Deeps, the cold black canyon that went straight down more than 150 feet. They talked too loudly and played their radios too loudly, and they defied gravity and physics with feats of daring and foolhardiness. They were saying, in their own way, Hey, look at me. Watch. Hey!

On the way home Ab and Bean took their time, poking at tar bubbles in the hot pavement and tossing stones at the windows of the abandoned schoolhouse down by the ball field, which had given way to tall grass and cat-o'-nine-tails.

"They say there's a tunnel between the Moses Webster House and the Winthrop House," said Bean offhandedly. He plucked a piece of grass and stuck it between his teeth.

Ab stopped in her tracks. "Who says?"

Bean shrugged. "Everybody knows."

"Where is it?"

"Nobody's ever found it."

"Then how do you know it's there?"

Bean didn't know. "Let's ask my mom. She's the one who told me."

"Well," said Mrs. Carver after a little thought, "I'm not sure where I heard that. It's just one of those legends you learn growing up on the island."

"Tell us about it, Mrs. Carver," Ab pleaded excitedly.

Bean's mom finished drying the dishes and hung the dishcloth to dry on the metal rack over the oil stove. "I'd love to, but I have to make a blueberry pie for supper tonight."

"We'll help," Ab volunteered.

Bean was less enthusiastic. "We will?"

Ab regarded him with a furrowed brow. "We will." She smiled up at Mrs. Carver. "And she can tell us while we work."

Mrs. Carver nodded and held out her hand to Abby. "Deal," she said. "You guys get the berries out of the pantry. They need to be washed and have the stems taken off. Pick out the white ones and put them aside with the stems."

Once everything was ready, Mrs. Carver began her story.

"Moses Webster and Isaiah Winthrop were business partners. They owned one of the granite quarries back in the mid-1800s."

"Which one?" asked Ab.

"I'm not sure," said Mrs. Carver. "I bet you could find out up at the historical society—Bean, just put in one cup of sugar, okay? I know the recipe says two and a half, but that's for cultivated berries. These little wild ones are a lot sweeter.

"Anyway, after some hard times, they finally got rich and decided to build the biggest houses on the island, side by side. So they made a friendly wager over who could build the biggest house. They agreed to keep their plans to themselves, and they agreed that a tunnel would connect the houses, so they could get back and forth easily. Especially in winter.

"Well, they hired crews and set to. Construction started on the cellars on the same day, and the tunnel was the first thing finished—Ab, would you get the pie pan for me? Anyway, as I understand it, Moses and Isaiah went off to Boston for the fall and winter. They had houses there, too—apparently there wasn't enough social life for them on the island in the winter—and when they came back in the spring, the houses were nearly finished.

"That's when everything started to go wrong. Apparently Moses's house was bigger in square footage and Isaiah's was bigger in height, so neither of them would concede that he'd lost the bet. Instead, Moses closed off his end of the tunnel and had another wing added to the back of his house."

"That's where my bedroom is," Ab chimed in.

"Right," Mrs. Carver agreed. "Isaiah closed off his end of the tunnel, too, and added another six feet to his tower."

"Did they stay in business together?" asked Bean.

"As a matter of fact, they didn't. Winthrop sold his shares to Moses Webster and went off and started his own granite company, right here on the island, to compete against his former partner.

"Neither of them ever spoke to the other again, although they lived in those houses, side by side, for the rest of their lives. I seem to remember that their houses in Boston were across the street from each other, too." Mrs. Carver sighed. "So sad."

She opened the heavy oven door, tested the temperature, then slid in the pie. "Now, why did you want to know all this? I suppose you want to start looking for the treasure."

"*Treasure*?" Ab and Bean replied in concert.

3

Widow of the Moors

"I THOUGHT THAT'S WHAT THIS WAS ALL ABOUT—old Minerva's treasure," said Mrs. Carver. She gently shut the oven door and set the wind-up timer on the stovetop.

"We don't know about any treasure," said Bean, as he emptied the stems and unripe berries into the garbage pail under the sink.

"Then what's all this about?"

Bean and Ab exchanged an unsure glance. "Well . . . ," said Bean tentatively.

Ab jumped in with both feet. "I've been hearing sounds in my room."

"Oh, really?" said Mrs. Carver. She finished washing her hands and turned off the water. "What kind of sounds?"

Abby told the whole story, with occasional additions from Bean whenever he felt that the telling was getting a little too dry.

"Very interesting, Abigail," Mrs. Carver said. She sat for a while, staring out the window but oblivious to the occasional passerby or the busy summer traffic down on Main Street. "Well, I'll tell you a little secret," she said at last. "When I was about your age, the Moses Webster House was empty—that was before the Johnsons moved in—and we'd go in the cellar sometimes to try to find the tunnel. I always felt we were just that close." She held her thumb and forefinger about a sixteenth of an inch apart. "But we never did find it. Neither has anyone else, as far as I know. If they did, they kept it to themselves, which would be impossible to do on the island."

"You mean, other people have tried to find the tunnel?" asked Ab.

"Oh, you bet they have. My father. His father. Probably most of the island has taken a crack at it one time or another." Mrs. Carver bent down toward her listeners. "That's the kind of thing you do with yourself when you don't have a movie theater or a video arcade." She laughed a light, warm, musical laugh that always made Bean smile. He'd never say it out loud, but he thought his mother was the most beautiful person in the world. His dad did, too.

"But what's the treasure?" Bean asked.

"That's the interesting part, I think," said Mrs. Carver dreamily. "It's romantic."

Bean rolled his eyes. "Oh, brother."

"Tell us," said Ab excitedly.

"Tell her," Bean suggested.

Mrs. Carver began. "It's very sad."

"I think I'll go clean my room and wash the dog," said Bean sarcastically.

"I didn't know you had a dog," said Ab.

"We don't," Mrs. Carver replied, looking at Bean a little sideways. "If you don't want to listen, you don't have to. But if you're going to look for the treasure, you'd better have all the facts, don't you think?"

Bean sat on the corner of his chair and resolved to listen with just one ear, until things got interesting.

"Well, Moses Webster had a son whose name was Reuben, and Isaiah Winthrop had a daughter, Rebecca."

"And they fell in love," said Ab enthusiastically.

"Right the first time," Mrs. Carver replied with a smile. "And—"

"And their fathers wouldn't let them see each other," Ab interrupted. "So they unblocked the tunnel, somehow, and met there in the deepest hours of the night."

"Don't you love the way I tell a story?" said Mrs. Carver dryly.

Bean was wondering if Ab maybe had an imagination after all.

"Am I right?" Abby begged eagerly.

"As rain," said Mrs. Carver.

"The treasure," Bean reminded her. "Can we get to it?"

"I am getting to it," his mother replied patiently. "Just a little more romance first."

Bean flexed his eyebrows, rested an elbow on his knee and his chin on his hand, and settled in for the long haul.

"As you might have guessed, Reuben and Rebecca ran away and got married, which made their fathers furious, so they disinherited them."

"What's 'disinherit' mean?" asked Ab.

Bean piped up excitedly. "That's when they take a sword and rip open your belly and take your insides out."

"Ooh, gross," said Ab.

Mrs. Carver shook her head. "Not quite, Mr. Shakespeare," she said. " 'Disinherit' means that they were stricken from the wills." Ab's face didn't register comprehension, so Mrs. Carver explained further. "People write up wills so that when they die, all of their possessions go to the people they choose."

"Like the melodeon," said Bean.

"That's right." Mrs. Carver turned to Ab. "When Bean's great-gram Johnson died, she left us her old melodeon."

"What's a melodeon?"

"It's a kind of organ that operates on air," explained Mrs. Carver. "You push pedals that open and close bellows inside, which pushes air through reeds. I wish it was here, but it's at my mother's house."

"That melodeon's over two hundred years old, and it's been around the world three times in an old sailing ship," Bean added.

"Right," said Ab condescendingly. "I'm sure it has." She looked knowingly at Mrs. Carver.

"This time he's not exaggerating," said Bean's mom. "Bean's great-grandmother's father was the captain of the *Barbara Day,* out of Gloucester in the last century. He wanted his family to sail with him, and one of the inducements he used was the melodeon."

"Did it work?" asked Ab.

"I guess so. They sailed with him 'til Gram J was full grown, at least three times around the world. After that, I'm not sure what happened. But the melodeon's been passed down through the family ever since. Anyway, where was I?"

"They were disinherited."

"Right. Reuben made his living at sea for a few years, also out of Gloucester, I think, while Rebecca kept house over in Owls Head where she could see the island. So, like many seamen's wives, she didn't see her husband but once or twice a year.

"Nevertheless, they managed to have a daughter, whom they named Minerva. Reuben would send her dolls from the ports he'd visit on his travels around the world. But then, one day, the dolls stopped coming."

"Shipwreck?" asked Bean.

Mrs. Carver shrugged. "Nobody knows. Reuben was never heard from again."

"Never?" said Ab.

"Never," Mrs. Carver replied, shaking her head.

"What happened to Rebecca?" Ab wanted to know.

"Well, she moved back to the island, into the cottage her grandmother had left her over on the creek—the little red one with the white trim where Litty Ames lives now. For a while Rebecca and Minerva seemed to get along fine. Rebecca's granny had left her some jewelry as well, and they managed to live off that. But Rebecca developed the habit of walking alone out on the moors on Lane's Island, usually early in the morning, even before the fishermen went out. Nobody knew it then, but that was the beginning of her madness."

"She went crazy?" said Bean.

"To put it bluntly, yes." Mrs. Carver replied. "But slowly. At first those few fishermen's wives who ventured out on the moors early to pick berries while the dew was still on 'em would find Rebecca sitting on Daddy Lane's Head, humming to herself."

Ab interrupted. "Daddy Lane's Head?"

"A little group of rocks that looks like a man's face if you see it from a certain angle, and use your imagination," said Mrs. Carver.

"Which Ab doesn't have," stated Bean, though with less conviction than he'd have said it not long ago.

"Bean," Mrs. Carver said sharply, "that's not nice. And it's not true. Just because Ab's imagination isn't like yours doesn't mean she hasn't any. She does. It's just different."

Ab stuck out her tongue at Bean, who reciprocated, with a smile.

"Children," said Mrs. Carver with a note of warning in her voice, "would you like me to finish the story later?"

Abby sat up straight. "No, please! I'm sorry. Go ahead. Bean will behave himself."

Mrs. Carver cleared her throat in a meaningful way. "Yes. Well, what began as Rebecca's gentle humming in time became an unearthly moan, punctuated by a chilling wail every now and then. Soon she just pined herself away and died of a broken heart. By that time she'd become sort of a legend. They called her the Widow of the Moors."

"I don't think I like this story very much," said Ab. "Everybody keeps dying. That's no fair."

"That's because it's not make-believe, Ab," Mrs. Carver explained gently, with a distant look in her eyes. "It's real life, and real life isn't fair."

"Still . . ."

"Want me to continue?"

Ab hung her head a little. She wasn't sure she did want to hear the rest. "Does it have a happy ending?"

"You'll have to judge that for yourself," said Mrs. Carver. "Besides, I'm not sure it has an ending yet."

"How can that be?" Bean objected.

"Because it's real life, and things that happen in real life have an effect on other people, sometimes many years later."

Ab wasn't sure she understood, but she wanted to find out. "Okay," she decided finally. "Carry on."

Mrs. Carver looked at Bean. "Okay?"

"Heck, sure," said Bean, with a good deal more confidence than he felt. "I got no problem."

"All right. Well, both Moses Webster and Isaiah Winthrop were somewhat shaken to their senses; at least that's the way it seems. Each of them decided to take Minerva, who was no more than two or three at the time, into his home.

"Of course, neither man would simply give in and let the other care for the child. In fact, the whole battle that followed had far less to do with Minerva than with the same foolish pride that had already destroyed their own children."

"What kind of battle?" said Bean, imagining at least a duel at sunrise.

"A legal battle," Mrs. Carver explained.

Bean was visibly unimpressed. "Oh," he replied flatly. Sometimes reality seemed such a waste of time.

"They fought for years. Meanwhile, Minerva shared her time between the two of them—back and forth, back and forth, from season to season across the narrow lane that separated the two great houses. And each grandfather would try to win her affection with money, or dresses, or jewels, all the while berating the other grandfather to her."

"Berating?" said Ab.

"Talkin' trash about him," Bean explained.

Ab looked at Mrs. Carver for verification.

Mrs. Carver nodded. "As a result, by the time Minerva was seventeen she had withdrawn into a world of her own, confining herself to the tower room of whichever house she was in, allowing only her trusted maid, Mary Olson—"

"Like Katie Olson?" Bean interjected.

"Katie's great-great-grandmother," Mrs. Carver affirmed with a nod. "Allowing only Mary Olson to serve her. Still, the grandfathers courted her affections with treasures, trinkets, and promises, for which she had no use."

"She wanted love," Ab declared.

"I think you're right, Ab," agreed Mrs. Carver. "Don't roll your eyes like that, Bean. They'll go back into your head and never come out again."

Bean's mother continued. "Finally, Mr. Winthrop died. As if to get in the last word, he gave all of his fortune and houses and businesses to his granddaughter."

"When was that?" asked Ab. Dates helped her keep track of things in her mind.

"Late 1800s," said Mrs. Carver. "Mr. Webster seemed to take exception to the fact that Isaiah Winthrop had beaten him to the grave, so he followed a few weeks later. Apparently he meant to deal with the situation in the next life. He, too, left his vast fortune in Minerva's hands."

"She must have been some rich, huh?" said Bean. "That's lucky."

"Oh, she was rich, all right," said his mother. "But lucky? I'm not so sure."

Ab cringed. "I don't like the sound of that."

Mrs. Carver continued. "Whether from years of habit or a kind of madness, I can't say, Minerva kept the same schedule she always had, moving back and forth from Moses's house to Isaiah's house—spring and fall at Isaiah's, winter and summer at Moses's."

"Weird," Bean observed grimly.

"Even after she got married?" Ab asked.

"She never got married. And she hardly ever went outdoors, except to cross from one house to the other, as far as I know, though there are stories that she wandered the streets late at night, dressed in black with her face veiled. That would have made her her mother's daughter, all right. But I don't think that part of the story holds much water."

"Double weird," Bean proclaimed.

"She had a number of servants, but the only one who saw her on a regular basis was Mary Olson. And Miss Minerva still kept herself to the two little tower rooms."

"Even with two great big houses?" Ab cried in disbelief.

"Mmm. And she'd conduct business from there—through Mary,

of course. She never spoke to anyone else directly, not 'til the end. But it seems she had a good head for business. The quarries did well right up until concrete took the place of granite as the building material of choice, just before the Depression. Then she plowed her fortunes into the fish factory, and that was still going strong when I was a little girl."

"She was still alive then?"

"Oh, no," said Mrs. Carver quickly. "I'm not quite that old. No. She sold the factory toward the end of her life. Closed the quarries and consolidated her fortune."

"That means she got it all together in one place, doesn't it?" asked Ab.

"Exactly right," Mrs. Carver replied. "And this is where the story gets really interesting."

"'Bout time," Bean grumbled, although he was actually spellbound by the tale.

"I said Minerva kept herself to the tower rooms; that's not entirely true. A year or two before she closed the quarry, she had two stonecutters come to the Moses Webster House; one was Italian and the other Swedish. There were a lot of Italians and Swedes working the quarries in those days. The odd thing was, these two men moved in, lock, stock, and barrel. The last that was seen of them, about two or three months later, was when Mary Olson took them down to the steamer ferry in Miss Minerva's best black carriage, pulled by four black horses in mourning."

"Mourning? What does that mean?"

"They were decked out as they would be for a funeral," said Bean.

"Spooky."

"That's not all," Mrs. Carver continued. "They were both dressed to the nines in top hats and tails of the finest silk. Mind you, these were men who'd probably never felt anything next to their skin but wool and burlap. But be that as it may. They got on the boat, and, according to postcards mailed from Boston about a week later, they were shipping out to the old countries. Then *pffft,* that was the last that was heard of them."

"Then what?" Bean inquired a little more breathlessly than he'd meant to.

"Then," said Mrs. Carver, lowering her voice theatrically, "the strangest thing of all. Packages began arriving from all around the world—day after day, week after week, from China, California, Greece, Italy, Spain, Russia, Persia, Patagonia—everywhere. Literally hundreds of these little bundles over the course of three or four years, all delivered to the docks by ships sailing from the four winds. They were picked up by faithful old Mary Olson and delivered to Miss Minerva in one of her little tower rooms."

"What was in them?" said Bean, nearly crawling out of his skin.

"Nobody knows."

"No," said Bean, "I mean at the end of the story, when she died. Somebody must have gone in and found all those boxes."

"Oh, they did," said Mrs. Carver with a little twinkle.

"Then, what was in them?" chorused Bean and Ab.

Mrs. Carver waited a little longer than necessary before she answered. "Nothing."

"Nothing?" said Bean and Ab, looking wide eyed at each other, then at Mrs. Carver.

"Nothing," she repeated. "Mind you," she added, opening the oven door, seeing the golden crust, and removing the pie, "there had been something in them. Mary Olson swore to that. Nothing very heavy, but something."

"Treasure," Bean said with a sigh.

"Treasure!" Ab echoed.

Mrs. Carver's head tilted indecisively. "Anyway, about the time the boxes started coming, Mary Olson began hearing footsteps on the stairs in the dead of night. One night she mustered enough courage to go find out who—"

"Or what," Bean interjected quickly.

" . . . was walking around that time of night. What do you think she saw?"

"Miss Minerva," Ab speculated breathlessly.

"None other."

"What was she doing?" asked Bean.

"Carrying a bundle down to the cellar. Nobody knows what was in it," Mrs. Carver added quickly in response to the question aborning in Bean's eyes. "But whatever it was, it was wrapped in blankets, and she was cradling it like a baby in her arms, and singing to it.

"What kind of treasure would she be singing to?" Bean mused aloud.

Mrs. Carver continued without answering. "Mary waited in her room, with the door cracked just far enough to see, until Miss Minerva came creaking up the stairs again, empty handed."

Mrs. Carver paused for breath. This time she wasn't interrupted. Bean and Ab were totally mystified, and looked it. She took some little satisfaction at having shocked even Bean to silence for once, however briefly.

She continued. "Whenever a package would come, this went on, night after night. Then came the oddest thing of all."

Ab didn't think that anything odder than this was possible.

"As time passed, fewer and fewer packages came until, finally, they stopped altogether. Then, one day, Miss Minerva sent Mary Olson out on an errand. A wild-goose chase, Mary called it. And while Mary was gone, Miss Minerva dismissed the other servants, all of whom found a generous bonus in their pay packets that month. When Mary returned, Miss Minerva was gone, too.

"Gone," Mrs. Carver repeated. "Without a trace. Nothing else was missing—no clothes, no food, no valuables. Nothing."

"Where did they find her?" asked Bean with trepidation, as if he had an idea of the answer.

"They never did." Mrs. Carver stood up and carried the pie to the counter.

"I knew she was going to say that," commented Bean.

"How do you know all this?" Ab inquired.

"Hearsay, mostly," said Mrs. Carver. Scent-laden steam curled from the pie as she cut it and the blueberry filling oozed out. "Seems Rebecca had kept a diary, which Minerva took over at some point—so both their stories were there in the same book. I think that's kind of poetic." A quick scan of her listeners' faces revealed that they didn't share her sentiment. "All right. Well, that diary constituted pretty much all of Minerva's reading. Many times she'd have Mary sit in the corner doing her knitting and mending while she read passages out loud. After a while, Mary knew long stretches of the diary by heart. Of course, the rest of the story she could fill in herself."

"And she told someone else. . . ," ventured Ab.

"Who told someone else, who told someone else," said Mrs. Carver. "And the story became part of island legend."

"I bet she was hiding some kind of treasure in the tunnel," Bean speculated. "That's why she had workmen at the house."

"Of course, that's what most people deduced," said Mrs. Carver.

"Which is why we used to go looking for the tunnel when I was a kid and the house was empty."

"Who inherited all her money?" asked Bean, cutting to what he considered the core of the matter.

"There wasn't any," said Mrs. Carver. "By the time she disappeared, she'd sold all the property. Even the houses were sold, with the new owners agreeing not to take possession until her death, or disappearance."

Ab was getting frustrated. "But the money had to go somewhere," she interrupted.

"Well, it turns out she spent it all on whatever was in those boxes. She spent probably hundreds of thousands of dollars."

"Maybe it was jewelry," Ab suggested. "That wouldn't have been too heavy."

"Maybe she didn't bury it in the tunnel. Maybe she left the island and took it with her," Bean added.

Ab picked up on the thread. "Maybe she moved to Europe with all her money and married a duke who was bankrupt but very much in love with her and—"

"Oh, please," Bean sighed, then asked indignantly, "Why haven't I ever heard this story?"

Mrs. Carver thought a moment. "You'd never have listened before," she said softly. "Too much romance." She sliced three juicy pieces from the warm pie.

"Who found the diary?" Ab asked.

"No one ever has," Mrs. Carver replied. "All we have to go on is Mary Olson's word that any of it is true—and she's been dead over eighty years. Of course, people always felt she knew more than she told, but one thing no one doubted—she was as loyal as the day is long. She'd have done anything for Miss Minerva."

"But she could have made it all up?" Abby said with alarm, bouncing to her feet.

"Could have," said Mrs. Carver calmly. "Who wants pie?"

4

"Every Work a Masterpiece"

"HERE SHE IS," Bean called from the opposite side of the graveyard. He was pointing at a white marble tombstone that leaned at a precarious angle due to its age and neglect.

Abby ran to his side, careful not to step on any graves along the way. She knelt at Bean's side and peered through a crust of yellow and brown lichen. "Mary, beloved of Hermann Olson, born October 1, 1843. Died April 19, 1917," she read aloud.

The sun was rich and dipped in gold, and the air was cool and slightly damp with a recent fog as Bean and Ab sat on the low stone border of the Olson grave. Abby absentmindedly traced the family name that had been embossed on the granite.

"I'm going to have a video tombstone," said Bean, as if that were a sensible thing to say.

Ab looked at him as if he'd just arrived from another dimension. "What are you talking about?"

"Interactive," Bean added, having had a second or two to think about it. "An infrared trip switch will make a video screen pop out of the ground when someone walks by." He raised his hands in the air. "And there'll be an interactive multimedia presentation so they can talk to me and ask me questions and find out how wonderful I am."

"How wonderful you were," Ab corrected.

Bean smiled impishly. "I'm flattered you think so."

Ab turned away and pretended to ignore him, but she couldn't keep from smiling.

"If only we knew what she knew," said Bean half to himself as he tossed a nod at Mary Olson's tombstone.

For a few minutes neither of them spoke.

In the treetops, crows called loudly to one another across the tiny clearing while the passing day drew long, dark shadows, like blankets, across the ground.

"Funny that no one's ever found that tunnel," Ab mused after a while. "I mean, if it really exists."

"They haven't looked the right way," Bean remarked philosophically.

"You mean they haven't looked in the right place."

"I doubt that," Bean replied. "Can't be that many places to look down there. I think they're just not looking the right way."

"I think you don't know what you're talking about," Ab stated. Slowly she tilted her head sideways, studying Mary Olson's tombstone from a different angle. "What's that?" she said, indicating some engraving barely visible above ground level and disappearing beneath the soil where the stone slanted.

"Writing," said Bean, pressing down the grass to reveal as much of the lettering as possible. "Lord, rest my . . . something," he read.

Abby began to dig away the turf with a brittle maple twig, but it kept breaking. "That's useless," she said, tossing it aside.

"Hey, wait," said Bean. "I've got an idea." He jumped to his feet and, bracing himself against the stone on the downhill side, began to push. Nothing happened.

"I don't think that'll work," said Ab. "It's been here too long. It's all grown in."

This was precisely the impetus Bean needed. Summoning all the strength he possessed, he wedged his feet against the low granite border and his back against the gravestone and pushed. This time there was a faint yielding.

"It moved," Ab cried. Scrambling to her feet, she got a good handhold on the weathered stone and heaved for all she was worth. Slowly, as if a dull old giant was being wakened from his sleep, the stone groaned to a somewhat upright position.

"Quick," said Bean, nearly out of breath, "get a rock and wedge it underneath."

"But if I let go—," Ab began in protest.

"I've got it. Hurry," Bean grunted mightily.

With that, Ab darted to the deeply rutted dirt road that ringed the cemetery and kicked a big stone loose from the side of the grassy ridge. It was larger than she thought, and by the time she wrestled it back to Bean, his face was bright red with the strain of his effort, and he was dripping with sweat. He didn't even have enough strength left to ask why she'd taken so long. Though he did think about it.

Abby stuck the rock in the opening under the tombstone, but it was too big. "Lift a little higher," she urged.

Bean looked at her as if she'd just grown another head. His eyes were bugged out and bloodshot, but, as bidden, he drew on his slim reserves and pushed the stone to a near perfect perpendicular.

That was all Ab needed. Working quickly, she dug a little hollow in the soft, dry earth just enough so she could cram the rock under the tombstone. Using both feet, she stomped on it until, finally, much to Bean's relief, it was wedged into the hole.

Bean fell on the ground in a heaving, panting pile of arms and legs, still unable to speak.

Ab bent down beside him to see if he was all right. When she saw that he was still breathing, she batted her eyes in gentle mocking. "My hero," she said, clasping her hands under her chin.

Bean started to say something, but Ab looked so ridiculous that all he could do was laugh. The sound of their joy silenced even the crows for a moment.

"Come on," said Ab finally. She rolled to the front of the stone and brushed away the crusted clumps of dirt. Bean got to his knees and crawled to her side.

"Lord, rest my bones as happy here, as she among her babes," he read.

Ab studied the curious epitaph. "What do you s'pose that means?" She read it again and shook her head.

Bean was thinking. "That reminds me of something."

"Huh?"

"Babes," said Bean. "Baby . . ."

They remembered together. "Cradling the package like a baby in her arms," they chimed with wide eyes.

"That's what Mary Olson said about Miss Minerva," Ab blurted out excitedly.

"She wrapped the bundles like babies and sang to 'em," Bean recalled.

Ab's forehead wrinkled in perplexity. "Babies? She was keeping babies in the cellar?"

Bean read the last line on the tombstone again. "As she among her babes." He looked aghast at Ab. "You don't think all those bundles—"

"Of course not," said Ab. "It's a clue. It means something else. It's a metaphor."

It was Bean's turn to be impressed, but he didn't say anything. "I know what that means," he said. He stood up and brushed off his hands on his jeans. "It's too weird."

"I'll tell you one thing," said Ab. "I don't know what all that babies stuff is about, but I'll bet you a quarter that the 'she' on the tombstone is Miss Minerva Webster herself."

"Must be," said Bean thoughtfully. "But what could 'babes' mean?" he asked as they walked the rutted road that led from the cemetery.

"What do you think?" said Ab.

"Some kind of code, maybe. You know how words can have more than one meaning."

Abby grabbed a green apple from a low-hanging branch and took a big, crunching bite. Immediately her mouth puckered and her eyes watered as the unripe fruit's sour juices touched her tongue. "Good apple," she proclaimed. Bean picked one for himself and joined her in the feast.

Neither of them said anything for a while as they trod the thick layer of gold that the setting sun had spread on the road. Bean chucked his apple core into the creek, where it landed with a *splop,* then bobbed to the surface, creating a pattern of concentric rings in the bright, still water. "She did know something, ol' Mary Olson."

The rumble of a motor troubled the silence. "I know that sound," said Bean, looking down the road behind them. "Uncle Phil." Bean stopped and waited for his uncle's familiar rusty yellow truck to come rattling around the corner. After half a minute or so, it squealed to a halt beside them. "Told ya," Bean said to Ab, beaming with pride.

"You kids want a lift downtown?" said Phil, but before the phrase was out of his mouth, they were clambering in back.

Bean and Ab both loved Uncle Phil, as did most of the kids in town. He was tall as a tree with salt-and-pepper hair that spiked out from his head in all directions, and he always looked as though he'd just climbed out of bed. Oddly enough, one of the legends that had grown up about Uncle Phil resulted from the fact that no one had ever actually seen him asleep. Not even his wife and daughter. When the fishermen gathered at the Donut Hole for coffee before going to haul at four in the morning, Phil was there. When the town gathered at the post office after the second ferry, Phil was there. Late at night, when everyone else was asleep, Phil's battered old truck could be heard driving back and forth all over town, like a watchman. In between, Uncle Phil was everywhere. He owned the only motel in town, so he spent lots of time fixing this or that, and he was a carpenter, and he sold insurance and real estate, and he owned a restaurant. He was poor as a church mouse and contented as a clam.

Since time immemorial, all the kids in town under twelve would gather at the flagpole every Friday night, then pile into the old yellow truck for a bumpy, blissful, crowded ride to Scooper's, the ice cream parlor on Harbor Hill. Phil would treat everyone to a single-scoop sugar cone of their choice. That was one of the reasons why all the kids loved Uncle Phil, but it wasn't the only reason. It was probably because he was a lot like a kid himself. That, and the fact that he was just the littlest bit mysterious, with a mischievous twinkle ever present in his green-gray eyes. Everyone called him Uncle Phil. But he really was Bean's uncle, his mother's brother.

Ab's and Bean's ride to town in the back of Phil's truck took only about a minute and a half. Phil drew to a halt near the bandstand. "Pile out," he called from the cab. The kids jumped over the side.

"Thanks, Uncle Phil," said Bean.

"Thanks, Uncle Phil," Ab echoed. It made her feel accepted as one of the family when he grunted in reply. "Ice cream tomorrow?" she asked.

"'Fraid not," he replied flatly. "Have to go off island again."

Bean knew what that meant. "Back to New York?"

Phil nodded. Unlike many islands on the Maine coast, Penobscot Island hadn't been overrun by tourists—not completely, anyway. So it still retained much of its charm as a working fishing village, and it was that very charm that for years had drawn artists from the world over to live there. Some famous, most obscure, some incredibly wealthy, some scraping by as carpenters and cooks, sacrificing everything for their art. All drawn by a certain irresistible magnetism that infused the island with an undefinable magic.

One of those artists was Maud Valliers, the dark, unfriendly loner who lived in the old Winthrop House, across the narrow lane from where Ab was staying. Maud had moved to the island about four years earlier and bought the Winthrop place, which, like the Moses Webster House, had stood vacant for years. Unlike the Moses Webster House, though, the Winthrop House was never reclaimed from the ravages of time. The paint was badly weathered, and green mold grew in the corners and places where the gutters had rotted through. Stonework was at odd angles, and the once-beautiful wrought-iron railings that adorned the roofs were broken in places and rusted away in others. Spooky as the Moses Webster House may have looked on a foggy night, it didn't hold a candle to Maud's place.

Spookier still was the woman herself.

Shortly after taking up residence, she opened a gallery on Main Street called Masterpiece and advertised that all of her paintings were guaranteed masterpieces. The gimmick worked, and her quirky paintings, all of which were covered with the letters *CB* in different sizes and styles (which Bean's mother called a terrible thing to do to a good painting) sold like hotcakes.

Pretty soon her work became popular in Boston. Then a prestigious gallery in New York began requesting her paintings. Because she never left the house herself, she struck a deal with Phil to have him run the pictures to Boston and New York in her car, which was left on the mainland, in return for a percentage of the sales price.

Soon the island's other popular painters began to take advantage of Phil's unique courier service. He didn't mind. The income supported all his other businesses.

"Are you leaving tomorrow?" Bean asked.

Phil leaned out the cranked-down window of his truck, with his nose resting on the crook of his arm. He leveled his unreadable eyes at his nephew. "First boat. Back Monday."

"Okay," said Bean cheerily. He was always a little uncomfortable under Uncle Phil's gaze. "Thanks for the ride," he said as he and Ab waved and started to walk away. But Uncle Phil didn't budge. He was thinking.

"How old are you, Beans?" he called after him. Phil was the one who bestowed the nickname Bean when Bean was no more than two years old. Not for any particular reason; he just liked the sound of it. Then the name caught on. But because Phil didn't like doing what everyone else did, he added the *s* and had called him "Beans" ever since.

"Thirteen," said Bean a little unsurely.

Phil studied him a little more. "Thirteen?"

Bean nodded.

Finally Phil sat up. "Hop back in. I've got something for you up at the house."

Bean and Ab dutifully jumped back in the truck and took their seats on the wheel wells. Bean shrugged in response to the question in Ab's eyes.

"Mom, guess what Uncle Phil gave me," cried Bean as he and Ab thundered up the wood walkway outside the kitchen door.

"Don't slam the—"

Slam.

"—door," Mrs. Carver finished with a sigh.

"Sorry," Bean apologized. "Guess what Uncle Phil gave me."

Mrs. Carver had been writing. She put down her pen and looked from Bean's excited face to Ab's excited face, then back to Bean, who was nearly bursting at the seams. "Well, I take it we can rule out a spanking," she said with a smile.

"C'mon," said Bean impatiently. "Be serious."

Mrs. Carver folded her hands in a serious manner and cleared her throat. "Sorry. Okay. Now, do you want me to guess, or are you going to tell me anyway? Because I think if you try to keep it in, I'm going to be scraping you off the walls."

"A motorcycle!" Bean blurted.

"A moped," Ab corrected.

Bean grabbed his mother's hand and pulled her out of the chair. "Come look at it."

Once again the screen door slammed as the kids herded Mrs. Carver outside. There, standing in the deep, velvety grass that Bean should have mowed three days ago, was what with a little imagination could be described as a moped. The tires were flat and the drive chain hung from the sprockets in a rusty knot. The rear-view mirrors dangled from the handlebars like broken limbs, and the headlight looked like Cyclops after his encounter with Ulysses. For some odd reason, the seat was in good shape, and there was still enough paint on the frame to suggest that the bike had once been blue and gray. The motor, however, was shiny with oil. When Bean turned the key and pushed the starter pedal, it hummed to life in a cloud of blue smoke, amid which Bean and Ab stood grinning like a couple of misplaced Buddhas.

Mrs. Carver smiled behind her hand as she waved away the smoke. "It's beautiful," she said with a cough. She recognized the bike as the remnant of a fleet that her brother had bought during his rental-business phase. Bicycles, outboards, mopeds; you name it, he'd rented it. As she recalled, it had been an expensive experiment, and before her stood its remains.

Bean brushed his hair out of his eyes. "It needs a little work," he allowed pragmatically. "But me and Ab can fix it up okay."

"Ab and I," Mrs. Carver corrected automatically.

The message was lost on Bean. "Well, you can help if you want to," he said skeptically. "You any good with duct tape?"

"That's not what I—"

"I can paint it," Ab volunteered.

There followed a brief debate about color. Ab's taste tended more toward pastels, whereas Bean favored Day-Glo orange.

"I think there's a can of blue spray enamel in the shed," Mrs. Carver suggested diplomatically. She had the comforting notion that Bean would soon lose interest in the project before the vehicle ever actually got on the road. "It's yours. No charge. Make sure you put newspapers down." She leveled a meaningful glance at Bean, but it bounced off.

While Ab painted the moped and herself blue, Bean fixed the mirrors and the headlight, patched the inner tubes, and repaired the chain. They worked by the porch light until well after eleven. By the time they finished, they had wheels—of a sort.

Once again they showed off their prize to Mrs. Carver, who was impressed by the work they'd done if not necessarily by the roadworthiness of the vehicle.

"Are you certain it's safe?" she ventured.

"Sure, what could be safer?" Bean declared unequivocally. "I just need to tune it up a little."

Mrs. Carver had a flash of inspiration. "Take it down to Alby Oakes at Carl's Garage tomorrow. He'll be able to tune it." Meanwhile, she'd have time to ask Alby to check out the bike for general reliability.

Now that they had done all they could, exhaustion fell. Abby, decorated with smudges of blue paint, dragged herself wearily up the sidewalk toward the Moses Webster House. Bean walked into the kitchen of his house, where he sat at the table for a long time. Eating homemade molasses cookies washed down with a glass of milk, he stared out the window at the resurrected machine glistening in the moonlight. "Ab said we should call her the Blue Moose," he said dreamily.

Mrs. Carver's gaze followed his out the window and came to rest on the bike. This was one of those special times she wished that Bean's father wasn't in the Coast Guard. Because of his repeated absences, sometimes for as long as three months at a stretch, it was hard for her to make decisions about things like this. During these times she had to be both mother and father to Bean. Right now the mother side was thinking it would like to throttle Uncle Phil, and the father side was saying, Oh, don't be such a worrywart. He'll be all right. You have to let him spread his wings a little. The longer she looked at the Blue Moose, the more it seemed that the mother side was going to win this argument. Well, she thought, if we're lucky, it won't pass inspection.

It was a little after two in the morning when Abby was stumbling down the cool hall toward her warm bed following her nightly trip to the bathroom that she heard the breathing again. Suddenly awake, she stopped short and listened. It was the same as always: long, low, and sad. She felt more than ever that the house itself was breathing—trying to tell her something. She could feel its exhalation like a feather on the tiny hairs at the back of her neck. Shivering from head to toe, she padded hastily down the hall and threw herself into bed.

The breathing stopped and she waited, holding the blanket just below her nose with both hands, staring into the dark. Sleep tugged heavily at her eyelids when, suddenly, the thumping started. She listened carefully. Where was it coming from?

There was only one way to find out. Slowly, fighting back a man-sized clump of fear, she drew the covers aside and put her feet on the floor. Why didn't anyone come running at the noise? she thought.

"They can't hear it," she reasoned aloud. "That means it's only at my end of the house." Not much comforted by this realization, she abandoned the safety of the bed and crept to the wall. Just as she placed her ear against the cold plaster, the thumping stopped. "Rats," she said aloud. She replayed the sound in her mind. "Top to bottom," she decided. She was sure of it. The sound had started near the ceiling, traveled downward in a straight line, and ended near the floor. It was a steady progression, and there was something metallic about the sound. Heavy, like iron. She'd heard the same thing somewhere before.

Where?

As she was deliberating, the noise began again. She nearly jumped out of her skin, but, recovering quickly, she pressed an eager ear to the wall. "Double rats," she exclaimed. It wasn't going from top to bottom. It was the other way around, and there was a lot more thumping. She moved along the wall to find where it was the loudest.

Just outside her room, on the left side of the hallway, was a closet. That's where the noise was coming from, she decided. Just inside the closet door.

Again the sound stopped. Ab held a trembling hand on the closet doorknob and turned it.

The door swept open silently, issuing a mothball-laden sigh of old air. A string hung alongside a bare lightbulb in the ceiling. She gave it a tug and the light came on.

The closet was fairly deep, with rows of hooks on either side from which hung an assortment of winter coats, hats, and scarves. Built into the back was a set of drawers as high as Ab's shoulders. The top of the dresser formed a deep, wide storage shelf, where piles of linens and blankets were kept.

To the right and left, the walls were covered with ancient, brittle wallpaper of an elaborate design. The rear wall, behind the shelf, was painted a dull, musty beige. There was nothing special about the ceiling, as far as Ab could tell. Same with the floor; cracked old linoleum had broken away in places, revealing wide pine boards with many coats of paint.

She tapped on the right-hand wall with the heel of her hand. Solid, no echo. Same with the wall on the left and the wall to the rear. All solid. No secret doors. No hidden rooms. "Triple rats," she said, shutting the door quietly. She went back to bed.

"There's gotta be something there," Bean insisted as they stuffed blue-spattered newspapers into a plastic garbage bag the following morning. Ab had told him her adventure of the night before, and they had just framed a plan to go investigate when Bean's mom reminded them to pick up the mess in the yard.

Ab had stopped stuffing and was reading: "Today's high, four degrees. Low, minus thirty-two."

Bean cast a quizzical glance. He was used to Ab's unexpected changes of topic. If he frantically referred back to something they'd been talking about earlier, sometimes days earlier, he could usually manage to follow the thread and make some sense of it. Other times, however, she'd say something right out of the blue, to which his customary response was "huh?" This was one of those times.

"Huh?"

Ab pressed the pages on the ground to flatten them out. "This says it's only going to be four degrees today."

"What's the date?"

It was Ab's turn. "Huh?"

"The date on the paper," said Bean. "What does it say?"

Ab found the date in the upper right-hand corner of the page. "March fifth, four years ago. Where'd you get such an old paper?"

Bean shrugged. "Mom saves 'em to start fires with."

"What kind of fires?"

"Fires. You know, to keep warm," Bean replied sarcastically.

Ab tilted her head a little sideways and thought a moment, taking in her surroundings. The huge forsythia bush in the little park across the sidewalk had always been green. She'd never seen it without its full, luxuriant robes of summer. The same of the maple trees: some a deep, dark purple, others an airy green. The same for the oaks, the alders, the birch, and the larch. To Ab, it was always summer in Maine. It was impossible to imagine the branches stark and bare against a steel gray sky, or the sidewalks and shore covered with thick layers of ice and snow. She'd never seen spring in full flower, when the lilacs and lupine seemed to try to outdo each other with gaudy displays of color and heady perfume. She'd never smelled the delicacy of autumn when trees were alight, each leaf a Viking king's death ship set ablaze for the journey to Valhalla.

For her, summer meant Maine, and Maine meant summer. Of course, other seasons came to Maine, but it was hard to imagine. When she slipped out of her daydream, she found that her eyes had focused on a small headline on one of the yellowed sheets of newspaper. "Priceless Collection Still Missing," she read aloud.

Bean looked up from his work. "What's that about?"

Ab read on. "Authorities appear no closer to solving the mysterious disappearance of over thirty masterpieces from Boston's exclusive Princep Gallery. The disappearance last month of the priceless original paintings was discovered by gallery owner Clifton Bright. As there was no sign of forced entry, gallery employees were early suspects. All but one, Amelia Williams, were cleared early in the investigation.

"Ms. Williams, who went missing the day of the theft and was at first believed responsible for the burglary, reported to work the following week, saying she had been on vacation and didn't know anything of the theft.

"A quick check of the employee records showed that, indeed, Ms.

Williams had long been scheduled for vacation as of the day of the crime. Subsequent investigation verified that she had booked into an exclusive hotel in Camden, Maine, and spent a week there. She was seen by many, including employees of the Maine State Ferry Service who attested to the fact that she had made several day trips to the islands of Penobscot Bay, primarily Penobscot Island.

"Most baffling, according to sources close to Bright, is the fact that one painting was left behind, Renoir's recently discovered *Weeping Widow,* perhaps the most valuable work in the collection. Other paintings in the gallery were blah, blah, blah . . . ," Ab synopsized: "It tells about the paintings. That's all."

"What's a Renoir?" Bean asked.

"He was one of those old painters," Ab explained.

"The one that cut off his ear?" Bean asked hopefully.

"No. That was van Gogh," said Mrs. Carver. She'd come out to inspect cleanup operations.

"Cut off his ear?" said Ab incredulously. "Why?"

Mrs. Carver leaned on the railing. "Passion, as I recall. He got in a fight with his best friend, another painter named Gauguin."

"He cut off his ear 'cause he had a fight?"

"Oh, don't be surprised. People will do anything for love: love of painting, love of a person. What would you say if I told you there was a man who ate a Porsche to show a woman how much he loved her?" said Mrs. Carver as she knelt beside them and helped stuff newspapers in the bag.

"Eat a porch?" said Bean skeptically.

"Not a porch, a Porsche. The car, you know?"

Now I know where Bean gets it, Ab thought, but she was too polite to say anything.

"When Uncle David lived in New Zealand back in the sixties, he read a newspaper story about a man who told this girl he'd do anything she asked him to. So she told him to eat a Porsche."

"Why?" asked Ab.

"Well, I think that was her way of saying 'Forget it,' explained Mrs. Carver. "But apparently he took her at her word."

"No, he didn't," said Bean, who sometimes had difficulty telling when his mother was pulling his leg. "Did he?"

"He did," Mrs. Carver asserted flatly. "He bought an old Porsche from the junkyard for fifty dollars and, piece by piece, from headlights to tailpipe, had the whole thing ground into a fine powder, which he sprinkled over his meals, like pepper. Took him three years to eat it all."

"Oh, well," said Ab, "I s'pose it could be done like that."

"Could and was," said Mrs. Carver. "Just goes to show, there's nothing people won't do—or at least try to do—when they're motivated by love, or hate. You'd be amazed."

A subtle motion caught Mrs. Carver's eye, and she looked up to see the curtain softly descend in the tower window of the Winthrop House. "You'd be amazed," she repeated softly.

"Did she marry him?" Ab wanted to know.

"'Course she didn't," said Bean. "Who'd marry somebody crazy like that?" He looked at his mother. "She didn't marry him, did she?"

"In fact, no," said Mrs. Carver. "The woman married someone else about three months after he started eating the car."

Ab was amazed. "Then why did he keep eating it?"

"He found out he could get in *Ripley's Believe It or Not* if he finished eating the car."

"Did he?" asked Bean excitedly.

"He did. I guess he hated to see anything go to waste."

5

The Discovery

"You're wasting your time," said Mr. Proverb. "From what I hear, half the people in town have tried to find that tunnel." He leaned across the table and lowered his voice to a whisper. "I've even taken a crack at it myself. Went over those walls with a fine-tooth comb. However," he said, slapping his knees as he stood up, "I guess at your age, your time is your own, so have at it. Just don't go knocking holes in anything. Okay?"

Ab and Bean thanked him, opened the cellar door, and flipped the light switch.

"Oh, I'm afraid the lights don't work," said Mr. Proverb. "Something's wrong with the wiring, apparently. I'm not surprised, it's so old. Amby Martin's coming to look at it next week." He took a flashlight from a shelf over the cellar stairs. "You'll have to use this, but be careful. There's all kinds of junk down there. I haven't got around to clearing it out yet. One of these days."

Ab followed Bean as he descended into the darkness.

"Have fun," Mr. Proverb called after them. "If you find any treasure, we'll split it, okay?" He laughed and closed the door.

Typical of most old island houses, the cellar of the Moses Webster House was formed by huge slabs of granite butted end to end, with the joists of the floor overhead forming the ceiling. "This is the biggest cellar I've ever seen," said Bean as they left one section and entered another through a low, wide door. It was also the deepest cellar he'd ever seen, with enough headroom even for his dad, who was six foot two, to stand up straight. However, as he and Ab entered the next section, the floor changed from granite slabs to dirt and rose steadily uphill, until they both were bending a little to avoid getting cobwebs in their hair.

To their right, the ground rose into darkness that Bean's light couldn't penetrate, but he could detect rough-cut granite pillars studding the ground and supporting the structure. Immediately ahead of them, a small rectangular window tucked under the joists admitted a weak wash of light.

"That's where they bring in the firewood," said Bean, indicating the window with his light and tracing a trail of old footprints and wood chips back to the pile of cordwood stacked against one wall.

Ab studied the wall, which was different from the others; it was plaster-covered brick rather than granite. "What's this for?" she said, slapping the wall loudly with the palm of her hand. "It doesn't even go all the way to the ceiling."

Bean traced it with the beam of light and came to a corner, where another wall, similarly made, led into the shadows at a right angle. "It's a cistern," he explained.

"A cistern? What's that?"

"Where they collected water back in the days before plumbing. Rainwater from the gutters ran down the spouts and ended up here. Then there'd be a pipe . . ." He stepped on tiptoe at the edge of the cistern and probed the shadows with the flashlight until he found what he was looking for. "There, see?"

Ab, too, stood on tiptoe and peered over the wall. "I see. So that went upstairs to a sink or something?"

"Right," said Bean, "where there was a pump." The beam of the flashlight bounded up and down as he mimicked the action of a pump handle.

"Listen," said Ab suddenly. "Footsteps."

Bean put the flashlight below his chin and shined it up into his face, where it cast long, unnatural shadows and made him look ghoulish. "Ooooo," he wailed eerily.

Shivers tripped up Ab's spine. She grabbed his elbow with one hand and slapped him hard on the back with the other. "Stop it!" she squealed.

Bean laughed and aimed the flashlight at the joists. "Somebody walking upstairs," he said casually.

Ab loosed his arm and slapped him again. "You stinker," she said, but she couldn't keep from laughing herself. "Let me have that for a while." She held out her hand and, reluctantly, Bean handed her the flashlight. "What's down this way?" she asked.

To the left, between the cistern and a retaining wall of granite, a narrow passage ran toward the outside wall on the side of the cellar facing the Winthrop House. At the end of the passage was a door with a small broken window covered with the grime of years. As Bean pushed, the door opened with a loud complaint, then thudded against the wall and nearly fell off its hinges.

They stepped through the doorway into a small, dingy room with a low ceiling and plaster walls that had once been painted white but were now a dusty gray. On the outside wall was a deep-set window looking out on the little dirt lane between the houses. Enough daylight seeped through the dirt-encrusted glass so the flashlight wasn't needed. Ab shut it off.

"What do you think this room was for?" she asked.

Bean made a thoughtful appraisal of the space. It was about six feet wide by eight feet long. Given the amount of debris on the floor—broken pottery and china, an old magazine and a newspaper, coffee cans full of cracked, dried paint, and assorted other junk—the room was most recently used primarily as a catchall for things on their way to the dump. "If it was closer to the stairs, I'd say they used it for storing preserves, or potatoes and onions, or apples, but it's too far away. And there ain't any shelves." Bean rubbed his hands along the walls. "Never were, either. No bracket holes in the plaster."

"Bracket holes?" Ab turned on the light and shone it on Bean's hands.

"If they kept food down here, they'd have had shelves, and if they'd had shelves, they'd have to have brackets, and if there were brackets," he concluded, "there'd be holes where the screws went that held 'em up. There ain't any."

Ab was impressed with his logic if not his grammar. Bean was making sense. "That doesn't happen very often," she said softly, looking at him with new eyes.

"What?" said Bean, only half listening. He was studying the wall.

"Oh, nothing," Ab replied. Bean stopped at a certain point and seemed to be tracing something with his fingers. "Did you find something?" she asked.

Bean continued a minute in silence, bending closer and closer to the wall and investigating something from floor to ceiling.

"What is it?" Ab asked impatiently.

"Grooves," said Bean softly. He went slowly around the room, running his hands over the brittle plaster, some of which fell to the floor at his touch. When he had completed his circuit of the room, he straightened up, put his hands on his hips, and leveled curious eyes at Ab. "There are grooves in the walls all around the room."

"Grooves?"

"Well, kinda grooves. More like scratches, I guess."

"What does that mean?"

Bean shrugged. "I don't know. Must mean something."

Ab scrutinized the marks for a few minutes. "There's no pattern," she pronounced finally. "Some of them are deeper than others. Some start above the floor. Some seem to start below it. Some are just a few inches long, and some go all the way from the floor to the ceiling. And there's no regular spacing between them." She stood up. "Maybe it's just the way they were made."

"Anyway," said Bean, "there's no place for any kind of tunnel or secret passage." He slapped the wall to his left. "The other side of this wall is where Mr. Proverb hangs his tools, and the whole thing is lined with workbenches. The porch is out there," he indicated the wall to the right, then rested a finger on the wall behind them. "This wall is backed by the cistern, and that"—he pointed at the wall facing them—"has windows in it. There's no place to put a secret door in here. Still . . ."

"Still what?"

"Well, if I was building a secret tunnel, this is just the kind of place I'd put it."

"Where it doesn't seem possible!" Ab joined in excitedly.

Bean nodded. "As I said, people have been looking the wrong way."

"They've been looking for something obvious," Ab agreed. "But if it was obvious . . ."

"Then it ain't much of a secret passage," Beam summarized with a sly smile. "That's right."

"So," said Ab, "since this is the one place a secret tunnel couldn't possibly be—"

"It must be where it is," they said in unison.

"Which means, there'd have to be some kind of lever or switch somewhere," Ab deduced. They conducted a scrupulous inspection for the next twenty minutes. They pushed everything that could be pushed. Pulled everything that could be pulled. Poked, kicked, and prodded everything in general until they were both exhausted. But nothing budged. Nothing even seemed as though it should budge.

"Well," said Ab reluctantly, "it seemed like a good idea."

Bean stepped to the window. "I'm hot," he said as he turned the latch and, tucking his fingertips under the lip, gave a sharp tug. Much to his surprise, the window shot up easily and slammed against the frame, dislodging one of the cracked panes and sending it crashing to the floor. Bean cringed.

"What's that?" Ab said with alarm, holding one hand on Bean's shoulder and the other across his mouth. "Listen."

"I don't hear anything," Bean mumbled through her fingers.

"That banging."

Listening carefully, Bean heard what she was talking about. The heavy, irregular, metallic thud was familiar to him. "Oh, that's just the weights," he said.

"Weights? What weights?"

Bean explained. "There are iron weights in the window casements, inside here." He tapped the wood frame to one side of the window. "They're connected to the window by a rope that goes over a little pulley up here." He pointed to the top of the window. "They make it easier to put the window up."

"Do it again," Ab commanded.

"Do what?"

"Close the window and open it again."

As Bean did so, the weights banged and thudded softly inside the casement. "That's the sound," Ab announced as she flashed a smile of triumph.

"What sound?"

Ab put both hands on his shoulders and squeezed, her eyes wide and dancing. "The sound I heard upstairs."

"You heard someone opening a window?" asked Bean, a little bewildered.

"No. It was much louder, much bigger sounding."

"Bigger sounding?"

"Oh, I don't know," said Ab in frustration. "Heavier sounding. But it was the same kind of sound. Like metal weights—great, great big ones—going up and down in the wall, in that closet in the hall."

Bean was having a hard time trying to catch up. "There aren't any windows in that closet," he recalled soberly.

"Not windows," Ab objected. "Put windows out of your mind. The weights are bigger, lifting something much bigger and much heavier . . . much, much heavier than windows." She waited for the realization to dawn in her companion's eyes.

When it did, they both yelled together. "The secret tunnel!"

"And I know where it is," said Bean.

"Where?" Ab's gaze followed his to the floor. He tapped his foot. "Right here," he announced confidently.

"What do you mean?" It was Ab's turn to be bewildered.

Bean ran his fingers lightly over the vertical grooves in the wall. "This whole floor lifts up—goes clear to the ceiling. That's why there are these scratches in the wall. Chips of plaster and dirt get caught at the edges when the floor goes up and down."

Ab gaped at him with wondering eyes.

"And," he concluded, "that's why it needs counterbalances."

"Counterbalances?"

"Those weights you've been hearing in the walls—great big ones—big enough to lift the whole floor."

"Then under here," said Ab, tapping the floor, "is the tunnel."

"Not only that," said Bean. "Someone's been using it."

6

Something Unexpected

"But who could it be?" asked Ab. "Not Mr. Proverb."

"No? Why not?" asked Bean.

"Well, you heard him. He said he looked himself," Ab protested.

"And what if he found it?"

"Then why would he let us come down here to poke around?"

Bean had an answer ready. "Because he didn't think we'd find anything. After all, nobody else has all these years."

"Then why wouldn't he just take the treasure to the bank, or whatever you do with a treasure?"

"Because everyone would know."

"So? It's his property."

"Is it?" said Bean mysteriously.

Ab furrowed her brow. "Isn't it?"

"That depends," said Bean. "The tunnel goes from this house to the Winthrop House, so who does it belong to?"

"Both?" Ab ventured.

"Maybe," said Bean.

The idea inspired another thought in Ab. "Then he'd want to move the treasure over here, to his property, so he could claim it all for himself. You men are so greedy," she added indignantly.

Bean was too busy following her train of thought to take offense, which proved, to Ab's satisfaction, that she was right in her assessment. "That's why the noises happen in the middle of the night. He's been going down when he didn't think anyone would notice, and moving a little bit at a time."

"There must be a lot of it," Ab deduced.

"But where is it now?" Bean queried aloud. "Where would I put a fortune so no one would find it?"

"I know," said Ab. She ran out the door with Bean in her wake and came to a stop at the cistern. Turning on the flashlight, she stood on tiptoe and looked over the retaining wall. "There are two compartments," she said as Bean's head appeared beside hers. She pointed the light at the mud floor of the compartment nearest them. "This one's empty. But that one," she aimed the weakening beam at the adjacent compartment, "is full of water."

The shaft of light struck the surface and, plunging into the blackened depths at a sharp angle, was quickly absorbed by the turbid contents. She shined the flashlight in Bean's eyes. "You've got to find out what's in there."

"Right," Bean replied facetiously. "And then she woke up."

"Oh, come on. You're not afraid of a little water, are you?" Ab cajoled. "Big Bad Bean doesn't want to get himself wet."

Bean smiled slyly. "Not at all. I'm just being a gentleman. Ladies first." He gestured grandly at the cistern. "I'll even give you a hand." He intertwined his fingers and made a step for her. "After you."

"Age before beauty," Ab retorted quickly.

"Don't tell me you're scared," Bean teased.

"Of course not," said Ab. "I have to hold the flashlight."

They both laughed.

"I know what to do," Bean decided at last. "I saw something back there." He scrambled off into the darkness. "Shine the light down here." Ab complied, revealing a long piece of loose copper pipe in the dirt. Bean picked it up, returned to the cistern, and thrust an end eagerly into the depths. "It's only four or five feet deep," he assessed. Ab followed his actions with the light, but the rapidly weakening beam penetrated the inky depths to only about a foot.

Bean probed the cistern carefully from corner to corner and in a crisscross motion across the bottom.

"Nothing there," he said, disappointment evident in his voice. "Too bad. It was a good idea."

"Where else could he put it?" Ab asked rhetorically. "There's gotta be a hundred hiding places down here." She shone the light into the shadows, but the beam had become too weak to make much headway against the darkness.

Just then, Bean thought of something.

"Hey," he said, dragging her back to the cistern, "shine that in here." He pointed at the empty compartment.

"The battery's almost dead," Ab remarked as she directed the feeble beam into the cistern.

"Mmm," said Bean. "I wonder what that means."

"What?"

"The walls are all slimy and wet. See the water line? This compartment's had water in it recently."

"So? Isn't that what it's supposed to hold?"

"Where did all that water go all of a sudden?"

"Man," Ab sighed. "We've gotta get out of here."

"Why?"

"'Cause we're looking for answers, not more questions. But that's all we're coming up with."

"Well," said Mr. Proverb as Bean and Ab emerged from the cellar stairs, "are we rich?" He was dressed in paint-spattered khaki coveralls and was coated with soot from the burner of the cast-iron kerosene stove he was fixing. In the light of day, it was hard to imagine anything very sinister about Mr. Proverb. In fact, it was all Ab and Bean could do to keep from laughing at their suspicions.

"No treasure," said Ab honestly.

"You don't use the old cistern anymore, do you, Mr. P?" Bean asked offhandedly.

"Shoot, no," said Mr. Proverb. "Hate to think what's in that old thing." He returned to his work. "Why do you ask?"

"Oh, just curious," Bean replied. "You don't see 'em much anymore."

"No," said Mr. Proverb from the bowels of the stove. "S'pose not. Well, maybe one day someone'll find that loot, and I can retire. Or at least hire someone to fix things for me."

"What kind of treasure do you think it is, Mr. Proverb?" Ab asked.

Mr. Proverb's laugh echoed inside the stove. "Probably Confederate greenbacks, with my luck. There's piles of that stuff turning up now and then."

"What was that little room off the cellar used for?" asked Bean. "The one with the plaster walls?"

Mr. Proverb stood up and scratched his brow with a sooty finger. "You know, I can't say. Seems strange there'd be a finished room way out there. I asked Eb Clark about it when we were looking at the place—he's the real estate broker who handled it. He had no idea, but he said he remembered hearing about a hallway that led to it once, right along the outside wall through my workshop. I keep meaning to look for signs of it, but it seems the only time I go down there anymore is to fix something. Oh, well. Another mystery. Hand me that wire brush, would you, Bean?"

Bean pulled the wire brush from the toolbox on the floor and passed it to Mr. Proverb. "What kind of signs?"

"Oh, I don't know, really," said Mr. Proverb, returning to his work. "Usually there's some kind of evidence when a wall's been moved or a structure's been changed. You just have to look for it."

"May we?" asked Ab ardently.

There was a muffled laugh from somewhere inside the stove. "Sure," came Mr. Proverb's distant-sounding voice. "Have at it. Just take care you don't break anything."

"Well," said Bean a little sheepishly, "we kinda did already."

Mr. Proverb was about to say something, but Ab jumped in with both feet. "A little window in that room. I forgot about it in all the excitement. We'll pay for it."

"I'm sure we can work it out," said Mr. Proverb. "Be extra careful from now on, all right?"

The kids agreed.

"You don't happen to have flashlight batteries, do you? These have just about had it," said Bean, shaking the flashlight.

"Nope. But there's another old flashlight in the third drawer on the left there." Mr. Proverb pointed blindly to his right at a narrow closet door. Bean opened it and saw a stack of deep drawers. He opened the third one from the top and found it full of odds and ends: mittens without mates, rolls of tape that didn't seem to have any beginning or end, keys for locks that probably no longer existed, and bits of rope too short to be useful but too long to throw away. Nestled among them was a battered old metal flashlight that didn't look as though it had much light left in it. Bean pointed it at his eyes and flicked the switch. Much to his surprise it came on. Much to his discomfort, it nearly blinded him for a few seconds. "It works," he said, rubbing his eyes.

"I still don't get what he meant by 'signs,'" Ab confessed as the beam of light played over the ceiling and walls of the workshop. "When you take out a wall, it's gone. Isn't it?"

"Maybe not," Bean replied unsurely. "If there was a hall along here, leading to that little room, it had to go through this wall." He indicated the wall behind Mr. Proverb's workbench; it was covered with large sheets of pegboard where tools hung in perfect array, each outlined with a marking pen. "But there's no way to get at it."

"I've got an idea," said Ab. "Come on." She grabbed Bean's hand and pulled him through the low opening between the sections and down the narrow passage between the granite wall and the cistern to the little white-walled room. "Here." She dragged him across the threshold and, slamming the door shut, slapped the wall against which the door had opened. "This is the other side of the wall. We just assumed it was an extension of the granite wall and we didn't notice anything special about it, 'cause it's plastered and painted white, just like all the other walls. But if a hallway ran through there once—"

"There's no granite," said Bean, jumping aboard the train of thought. "Just lath and plaster. . . . I'll be right back."

Ab waited in the dark for what seemed like hours but was only two to three minutes. When Bean returned, he was carrying a hammer and a nine-inch spike. "I found these in the workshop," he said.

"What are you going to do?" said Ab worriedly.

"I'm going to try driving the spike through the wall. If it works, we've proved our theory. If it doesn't . . ." In one swift motion, he dropped to his knees, placed the spike at a right angle to the base of the wall, and drew back the hammer.

"Hold it," cried Ab, catching her breath. "You can't do that. Mr. Proverb said—"

"I already asked him," interrupted Bean, giving the spike a mighty whack that created a tiny explosion of sparks. "He said okay, as long as we clean up any mess I make." With a big smile, he delivered another blow, then another. Each concussion generated a shower of plaster. The larger pieces settled to the floor, but the dust floated in the air, making the room seem murky in the weak light that slanted through the window.

But the wall didn't give.

"It must be granite," said Ab dejectedly.

"No," said Bean, who had worked up a sweat with the fever of excitement and the strain of his effort. "It's gotta be here," he said with another blow. "It's gotta be." Another blow.

Ab was afraid he was getting out of control and might hurt himself. "Bean, it's all right. We were just wrong, that's all." She patted him on the shoulder. "Settle down."

Bean wasn't listening. One after another he delivered harder and harder blows on the spike. Twice he missed and hit the wall. Once he hit his hand and yelled in pain, but it only seemed to make him that much more determined. Finally, with all the strength he had left, he delivered a resounding smash dead on the head of the spike. An explosion of sharp red chips and dust issued into the white-walled room. He stopped suddenly.

"What's that?" said Ab, bending to pick up one of the pieces, which she inspected closely. "It's brick," she said, answering her own question.

Bean drew his sleeve across his brow and let the hammer fall to the floor. "Brick?"

Their eyes lit up simultaneously. "It's been filled in. There was a hallway here."

7

Trapped

"Well, you two are turning into quite the detectives," said Mrs. Carver when they had told her what they'd been up to and what they'd discovered. "Imagine, the whole floor coming up. No wonder we've missed it all these years. Who'd've thought . . ."

"Now all we have to do is figure out a way to open it," said Ab.

"There's got to be some kind of switch or something," Mrs. Carver theorized. "Somewhere. But wherever it is, I bet it's well hidden."

"Well, it's not in the room," said Bean. "There's not much there, and we've tried everything."

"Nevertheless," replied his mom, "if your theory is correct, there has to be a switch of some kind that sets the mechanism in motion."

"It's been a long time," said Ab. "What if it's not there anymore? Maybe that's how they sealed the tunnel—old Moses Webster and Isaiah Winthrop. They just took out the switches."

Bean and his mom nodded. "Could be," said Mrs. Carver. "That would be great."

"Great?" cried Ab. She didn't think so. "Why?"

Mrs. Carver uncovered a steaming pan of buttered carrots and pushed them across the table to Bean. "I saw you put those carrots back. Now, take twice as many out and eat every one of them."

"Oh, Mom," Bean protested. "I hate cooked carrots."

"I know you do," Mrs. Carver replied with a smile. "That's why I make you eat them. It builds character."

"Or 'carrot-er,'" Ab interjected with a giggle.

"'Carrot-er,'" Mrs. Carver repeated. "I like that."

"Hilarious," mumbled Bean. "Two of them. Just what I need."

"You know you love us," said his mom, giving him a hug.

Bean turned bright red. Not because of the hug, but because there was something in the remark that made him uncomfortable, though he wasn't sure what or why.

"Anyway," said Mrs. Carver, ladling a heap of carrots onto Bean's plate, "it's great because if they removed just the switches, the guts are probably still in place."

"The guts?" said Ab tentatively.

"The insides," Mrs. Carver explained. "Let me give you an example. If you tore that light switch off the wall and plastered over the hole and papered over the plaster, all you've done is hide the wires. They're still behind the wall, just waiting for someone to put in a new switch. As long as the wires are getting power from somewhere, they'll work."

"I see," said Ab. "So the guts that make the thing work must still be there somewhere."

"Must be. That's why you've been hearing the weights. The mechanism still works, and somebody's using it," Mrs. Carver concluded. "Anyway, it's a thought."

"But we've got to find it first," said Bean, with his last mouthful of carrots that he was trying to swallow without tasting. He found that holding his nose helped, but his ears popped when he swallowed.

"That's the challenge," said Mrs. Carver as she rose from the table and began to clear the dishes. "That's where you prove if you're real detectives, I'd say."

The night was dark and clear, and the air was thickly scented with the sweet, pungent smells of summer, but all this went nearly unnoticed by Ab and Bean as they made their way up the back steps of the Moses Webster House. In the kitchen, the teakettle simmered lazily. Mr. Proverb must have fixed the old kerosene stove. Other than the gentle hissing and the rhythmic ticking of the dining room clock, all was silent.

A few soft lights had been left on, making islands of illumination amid the relaxing ocean of soft shadows.

"Where is everybody?" asked Bean as he fished the old flashlight from the drawer.

"There's a concert at the church tonight," Ab replied, opening the cellar door. "Remember? The whole town's up there."

Bean remembered seeing notices in the store windows downtown: "String Quartet in Concert." It wasn't the kind of thing he got excited about, but it kept the summer people off the streets. Of course,

Ab was a summer person, too, but she was different. "Oh, yeah," he said blankly. "Well, that's just as good. Nobody to bother us."

Truth be told, though, as Ab and Bean trod warily down the creaky cellar stairs, neither was comforted by the fact that no one else was in the house. But they put on a brave face, swallowed their fears, and followed the flashlight's bright beacon to the little white-walled room.

"I still don't see anything that could be a switch," said Bean. He scanned the walls, the ceiling, the floor, and the corners with the light. He closed the door and inspected the strip of wall behind it as well as the door trim and rough molding. "It must be someplace else."

All at once, there was a tremendous rushing noise accompanied by the faint movement of air in the still darkness. "What's that?" Ab cried, her heart leaping to her throat.

Bean stood and listened. He knew that sound, but it was so out of place. "A fountain?" he hazarded.

It sounded like cascading water. "The cistern," said Ab, reaching for the door. But before the words were out of her mouth, there was a shudder in the floor that, just for an instant, froze them in their tracks. "What did you do?" Ab wailed.

Bean shone the light in her eyes. "I didn't do anything," he said defensively. Suddenly, the floor began to rise. "Let's get out of here," he yelled.

The delay was costly. Ab grabbed the doorknob and yanked it. The door opened half an inch, then stopped, unable to swing farther inward because of the floor, which was rising steadily. "It won't open," Ab screamed, fear shaking her voice. "It won't open."

Bean flung himself at the grimy old window, although he knew it was far too small, even for Ab. He pounded on the glass until one of the panes cracked, then he knocked it out and began calling into the night. But there was no reply, and all the while the floor kept rising, inexorably, until their heads were just inches from the ceiling. He stopped shouting and Ab took his place at the window, screaming for all she was worth. Surely, thought Bean, someone would hear that.

At last she stopped. No response. None.

By this time they were on their knees, bending their heads in the three feet or so between the floor and the ceiling. "There's the sound," said Ab, holding up a finger. Sure enough, the counterweights could be heard in the walls above; they were a hundred times thicker and heavier than the window weights, but unmistakable.

It was all academic now. Within thirty seconds they would be crushed like bugs against the ceiling. They lay on their backs, panting, staring at the feeble glow from the flashlight as it got smaller and smaller and brighter and brighter as the ceiling came toward them.

"I'm sorry I got you into this, Beanbag," said Ab hoarsely. "I didn't know it would end this way."

The ceiling was less than an inch from their faces now. Soon it would all be over, but Bean had something to say first. And nothing was going to keep him from saying it.

"Abby?" he said softly. He never called her Abby.

"Uh-huh."

"I just want you to know something."

"What?"

"Well, I just want you to know that I—"

With a sharp thud, the floor stopped moving.

"It stopped," cried Ab. Bean waited. It could just have caught on something. But no, the water had stopped running into the cistern. "That's how it's done," he said, bumping his head sharply against the ceiling as he started to get up. "Ow!"

"Lie still!" Ab admonished. "What are you talking about?"

"The mechanism is hydraulic."

"Hydraulic?" Ab asked.

"Yeah. Powered by water. Did you notice how the floor stopped moving at the same time the water stopped flowing in the cistern?"

Ab suddenly realized that the water had stopped. She nodded.

"Somehow the force of the water, or the weight of the water flowing from one compartment to the other, is what runs the counterweights or pulleys that move the floor. That's why the empty tank was so wet." He studied the large slabs of granite that made up the walls. "There must be a huge holding tank of some kind outside the walls," he speculated.

"But who made it work?" said Ab shrilly. "There's nobody here. I know the Proverbs are at the concert. They went with my folks, and so did the rest of the guests." She paused a moment. "What are we going to do now?"

"Wait," said Bean.

"Wait?"

"What goes up . . . , " said Bean.

"Must come down," Ab concluded.

For a minute or two they entertained their own thoughts.

"Bean?" said Ab at last. Her voice had lost its hysterical edge; just a faint tremor remained.

"Mm?"

"What were you going to say?"

Bean felt his face redden, and little prickles seemed to crawl up the back of his neck. He was glad his face was in the shadows. "What?"

She repeated the question.

"Oh," said Bean, playing for time. There was nothing he wanted more than to say what was on his mind, but it would take another encounter with death to drag it out of him. "I don't remember. It's not important."

"Not important?" Ab echoed.

Bean wondered if there was a trace of disappointment in her voice. Maybe. Maybe not. Who knows with girls?

The silence was suddenly broken by the sound of rushing water. Instinctively, Ab and Bean braced themselves. The floor should begin to go down, but what if. . . ?

Within seconds they relaxed. The floor shuddered once again and began to move away from the ceiling. Ab let out a relieved sigh and pushed against the ceiling, as if to assist the mechanism in its operation. A minute or so later, they were on their feet again. The instant the floor descended past the bottom edge of the door, Ab tugged it open and jumped out into the corridor, followed closely by Bean. He leapt to the cistern and shined the light in, just in time to see the last trickle of water leave the empty section.

"It's like a big toilet," he said, "divided into two parts. But there has to be a supply of water coming from outside somewhere." He flashed the light across the earth and granite walls to the rear of the cistern.

"Why?" said Ab as she dusted herself off. What she really wanted to do was rush up to the church, find her mother and father, and throw herself into their arms and cry. But if Bean was going to stick around, acting as though nothing had happened, so was she.

"Because otherwise this would be a perpetual-motion machine," said Bean learnedly. "And there ain't no such animal. There." He turned the beam on a two-inch-wide pipe at the back of the cistern. "There's probably a natural spring around here somewhere."

"I've never seen one," said Ab.

"You wouldn't," Bean replied. He handed her the light and began to brush himself off. "It's underground." He took the light again and trained the beam into the empty cistern. "All we need to do now is find the jigger."

"Jigger?"

"You know, the jigger. The thing you flip to flush a toilet."

"That's called a jigger?"

"Yeah—what do you call it?"

Ab thought a second. "The flush button?" That didn't sound right. "I don't know. I've never called it anything—you just flip it. It doesn't have a name."

"Yeah, it does," Bean insisted. "It's a jigger. And somewhere around here there's a great big one. And where there's a jigger, there's a float." Once again he flashed the beam around inside the cistern. After a few seconds, it fell on a large glass ball connected to a long metal arm that disappeared through a slot in the tank wall.

"There it is," he said.

"What does it do?" asked Ab.

"Shuts off the water supply when the tank gets full."

Bean shone the light on a large brass disk in the bottom of the cistern. The floor sloped slightly toward the disk from all directions. "There's the drain. The water must run into some kind of underground system."

An ancient arm and elbow arrangement of brass rods was affixed to the near edge of the metal disk. Bean explained the mechanism to Ab, who caught on quickly. When pressure was applied to one side of the disk, the other side lifted up to let the water out. Ab immediately took the flashlight from Bean and played it about the floor until she found the length of pipe they had discarded earlier in the day. Seizing this, she handed Bean the flashlight and began to poke at the depths of the full cistern.

Bean was perplexed. "What are you doing?"

"If this side has a plug like the one on that side, and I can somehow find one of the rods and push it down, it'll flush. Right?" Once she knew what she was looking for, it didn't take her long to find it. "There it is," she said, and Bean flashed the light toward it. "Now all we have to do is . . ."

Using both hands, she pushed straight down on the rod. Immediately, water began to rush into the empty section and out of the full section in a swirling, hissing whirlpool. A heavy rumble added to the cacophony, announcing that the hidden mechanism was at work.

“Look,” Bean cried, shining the light into the little white-walled room.

Ab rounded the corner of the cistern and, with widening eyes and a thrashing heart, watched as the heavy stone slab—nearly four by eight feet—began to rise, revealing a deep, dark rectangular hole cut in the bedrock, like a tomb.

8

Everyone on Earth Is Out of Town

By 2 A.M., Mrs. Carver was frantic. Bean and Ab hadn't been seen since just after supper. Of course, the first place she had looked was the cellars of the Moses Webster House, which she and Mr. Proverb ransacked by candlelight, because he couldn't find his flash-light. But there was no sign of them. Not a sound. After that, Mr. Proverb called Constable Wruggles, who called Tiny Martin, chief of the volunteer fire department. The alarm went out until the whole town was out and about, searching the waterfront, the quarries, the woods, and the granite slag heaps.

By dawn, no one had turned up the least sign of Bean and Ab. It was as if the earth had opened up and swallowed them whole.

Which it had.

"Turn the light on again," said Ab. Bean started to protest, but she cut him short. "I know we need to save the battery, but just a minute won't make any difference. It's so black in here. I have to see some light."

"But—"

"Just for a minute, Bean," Ab pleaded. "Come on."

Bean relented. There was a soft click, and a feeble light filled the chamber with an eerie luminescence and huge, irregular shadows. Weak as it was, the light was such a stark contrast to the bottomless darkness they'd become accustomed to that they rubbed their eyes.

Ab glanced at her watch. It had been nearly nine and a half hours since they had stumbled down the steps beneath the floor and the huge stone slab had descended silently over their heads. They had panicked and hollered and screamed and cried and pounded the walls and ceiling until their hands were raw and their ears rang with the sound of their own hoarse voices. In that nine and a half hours, Ab had mentally kicked herself a thousand times for their foolishness.

Now they were tired and hungry, and the heart-stopping thunder of fear had given way to deep, tightening knots of despair in their stomachs.

Bean couldn't stand to see the tear stains on Ab's face or the hurt, hopeless look in her eyes. He shut off the light.

"We'll never get out of here," Ab said for the hundredth time. It had become a refrain that, after a while, Bean ignored. It did no good to argue. "This place has been hidden for a hundred years, and we found it only by accident." Her voice trailed off into sobs, between which she choked out the words of prophecy. "One day, another hundred years from now, they'll find us here. Dusty and moldy."

"Oh, stop it, Ab," Bean scolded sharply. "We're tired and hungry and scared, is all."

"Oh, thanks. I'd almost forgotten I'm starving to death," Ab snapped. "Remind me again in a couple of hours."

Bean felt a curious rage that he didn't know what to do with, so he stifled it. No matter what he said, Ab would turn it on him somehow.

Once again they were entombed in silence.

"I'm sorry, Bean," Ab whispered at last.

Bean made his way to her in the dark, sat down beside her, and put his arm around her shoulders. He'd been waiting a long time to do this, to give her comfort. She leaned into him and, burying her face in his jacket, wept silently. He sat stiff as a board, afraid to move for fear of breaking the bond between them. He patted her shoulder softly.

"It's okay," he said. "They're looking for us. Mom knows we're here. I bet we'll hear them digging any minute now." Inside he was wondering what was taking them so long.

"At least we have air," said Ab between sobs. "That's something to be thankful for."

"What an idiot!" Bean cried, leaping to his feet.

"Who are you calling an idiot?" Ab replied, a heavy concentration of warning in her voice.

"Not you," Bean explained hurriedly. "Me." He clicked on the light again and, holding it close to the wall, played it carefully along the corners where the walls met. "Of course, air is getting in here somehow."

"So?" Ab rose to her feet and pressed her nose into the halo of light.

"So, if air can get in, there's a way out," he deduced.

Ab's heart sank. "If there was a place big enough for us to crawl out, we'd have seen it by now."

"I know," said Bean, who was sticking his face into corners and seemed to be sniffing. "But maybe something can get out. Like a wire or a stick—something big enough to attract attention. Look around and see what you can find."

Abby shuffled her feet through the deep shadows. The floor was as bare as if it had been swept. "There isn't anything," she said morosely at the conclusion of her search. Then something occurred to her out of the blue. "Wait a second. I've got a piece of paper . . ." She felt frantically through the pockets of her coveralls. "And a pen. We can write a note and slip it through the crack." She paused. "If we can find a crack, that is. What are you sniffing for?"

"I'm not sniffing," said Bean quietly. "I'm trying to feel anyplace where air might be coming in." He drew a quick breath. "And here it is. Put your hand up here." He grabbed Ab's hand and pulled it to a place in the far corner. "Feel that?"

Ab closed her eyes and mentally focused all her senses on her fingertips. "I do," she cried. "I can feel it!"

"Here, you take the light and write a note while I see if I can dig out the dirt to make the crack a little bigger." He handed her the light, which was dying fast. She sank to her knees, spread the fragment of white lined paper against her thigh, and began to write. The instant she finished her note, the light flickered one last time and went out.

"Here," she said, handing the flashlight to Bean. "Dig with this. It's not good for anything else."

With the aid of the metal casing, Bean was able to chip a seam of plaster from the corner. "That's funny," he said as the fragments fell to the floor.

"What?"

"I don't see any light, but the air is coming in faster than ever."

"What does that mean?"

Bean wasn't sure. "Let me have the paper anyway," he said, feeling for Ab's fingers and taking the slip from her. "This opening goes somewhere, and if there's someone on the other side, they'll find the note." The paper fit easily into the crack and, with a little tap, fell through to the other side.

Bean slid slowly down the wall until he was sitting on the floor. "Now, we wait."

"And pray," said Ab, sitting beside him. She put her head against his shoulder. When he put his arm around her, she felt less helpless.

A little less helpless.

Soon they were sound asleep.

"What was that?" said Ab, waking with a start.

Bean rubbed his eyes in the darkness. For a few seconds he forgot where he was. Then he remembered, and his stomach tied itself into a sickening knot. "Ab?" he said sleepily. "Did you say something?"

"Yes," said Ab, scrambling to her feet. "I thought I saw something. A light."

Bean stood up and tried with all his might to pierce the thick darkness. Nothing. "You must have been dreaming."

"I'm sure I was awake," Ab protested, though she wasn't really sure. In that darkness, it was hard to tell where sleep stopped and waking began. "I'm sure of it," she added, this time with a little less conviction.

Bean felt there was no point in arguing. In fact, it might give her another flicker of hope if she could convince herself she had seen a light. "Well, maybe you did," he said. "What did it look like?"

Ab tried to remember. She'd been so sleepy. "It was like a flash," she said, then thought better of it. "No, more like a sweep."

"A sweep?"

"You know, like a lighthouse lamp on a foggy night," Ab explained. "Whoosh. It sweeps by, then it's gone. Very weak, though."

"How many times did you see it?"

"Two or three," she speculated. "I must have been half awake. I saw the first one and it woke me up all the way. Then a couple of seconds later, I saw the next one. Then another. I know I did."

"It must have come from up here," said Bean, squinting at the narrow crack he'd pushed the paper through. He put his eyes as close as possible to the crack and immediately was met with a faint flush of anemic light. "Hello," he cried at the top of his lungs.

"What are you doing?" said Ab, the adrenaline suddenly pulsing through her.

"I saw it," Bean cried. "You were right. I saw a light. Hello. Help . . . help! We're in here."

Instantly Ab was beside him, screaming as loud as she could.

They stopped and listened. No response. If they tried hard, they could imagine sounds in the remote distance, but it was no more than the sound of their own hearts beating.

Again they screamed until tears stood in their eyes and sweat ran down their faces.

Again, not the slightest whisper of reply. The light was gone. Perhaps they'd only imagined it after all.

Dejected and breathless, they sank once again to the floor, but no sooner had their tired bones settled into place than they heard the now familiar sound of cascading water. Distant. Ever so distant. But unmistakable.

"It's the cistern," Ab cried, pulling herself once more to her feet. Bean was right behind her. Together they stared hopefully toward the ceiling as, ever so slowly, preceded by a whistling rush of air, it began to rise.

They didn't wait for it to ascend all the way. As soon as there was room enough to scrape through, they helped each other scramble up the steps and over the edge onto the cellar floor.

Once they were out, the floor continued its mechanical journey toward the ceiling of the little white-walled room as the cistern filled behind them. No sooner had the floor come to rest than the cistern began draining and the floor descended noiselessly back into place. Bean and Ab stood watching, their eyes closed to narrow slits against the morning light and their senses numb with a flood of conflicting emotions as their former dungeon disappeared from sight beneath the great granite slab.

For a minute or so they stood staring. Then the rushing water slowed to a trickle, bringing them to their senses. At the same time, they realized they were holding hands. Quickly, with reddening faces, they shook free of each other.

"It's daytime," said Ab. "My folks will freak."

"So will my mom."

Still, they stood for a moment, nearly drowned by the waves of relief and confusion and leftover fear that swept over them. But something had happened down there, something that would change their relationship forever. Something that would take a lot of time to work itself out.

"Where is everybody?" said Ab as she thundered down the stairs, nearly colliding with Bean, who had been calling from room to room on the first floor. "There's nobody here." She glanced at the clock. "And it's only six o'clock."

It was the same story at Bean's house. His mother was gone, and her bed hadn't been slept in.

An eerie silence greeted them as they emerged onto the wood walkway. Usually at this time of day, Main Street was bustling with the traffic of carpenters and shopkeepers on their way to work. Across the deserted street, the coffee shop door stood open, but none of the early risers who usually packed the place were there. Instead, plates on the tables were heaped with half-eaten breakfasts. Coffee still steamed in cups, and a kettle boiled furiously on the stove at the back of the room, but there wasn't a soul to be seen.

"Grady," Bean called, running to the kitchen, but Grady, whom Bean had never seen outside that kitchen other than at Thursday night beano at the Legion Hall, wasn't there. He had been. The signs of his cooking were everywhere. Bean grabbed some blueberry muffins from the tray on the counter. They were still warm. "We'll pay for these later," he said as he handed one to Ab, who immediately began devouring it. They went back onto the street again.

There was nobody at the garage. Or at the parking lot. Even the old men who seemed to live around the potbellied stove in the hardware store, and were as much a fixture of island life as the granite itself, were gone.

Out in the harbor, all the boats tugged at their mooring lines, seeming anxious to be about their day's work, but there were no lobstermen to man them. It was as if everyone on the island had disappeared in the midst of their daily routines. Everyone except the two of them. Ab threaded her arm through Bean's. She needed the reassurance that he, too, wasn't going to disappear.

"Bean," she whispered, "what's going on? Where is everybody?"

9

The Secrets of Maud Valliers

BEWILDERMENT WAS JUST ABOUT TO GIVE WAY TO PANIC when a sound was borne to them on a contrary breath of wind, freezing both Bean and Ab in their tracks.

"Did you hear that?" said Bean.

Ab was already off, running down the sidewalk. She called over her shoulder. "It was a voice. This way . . . somebody's down this way. Come on."

Within seconds Bean was beside her. The slapping of their sneakers on the sidewalk echoed eerily from the vacant buildings, but in the distance the voice was growing louder. "That's Tib Wruggles," said Bean once they were near enough to make out a word now and then.

"The constable?"

By now they were abreast of the bank and were able to see where the voice was coming from. It was a sight that brought them to an abrupt halt.

The whole town, it seemed, was pressed in a compact semicircle around Bickford's flatbed truck in the parking lot of the fire station. Even from a distance, Bean and Ab could make out Ab's mom and dad, the Proverbs, and Bean's mom standing stiffly and nervously on either side of Constable Wruggles, who was speaking to the crowd through a bullhorn. Mrs. Carver was wringing her hands, and Mrs. Petersen was drying her eyes on the hem of her sweater.

It seemed like a dream as Ab and Bean took to their heels again. "Mom!" Bean shouted. But they were still too far away, and Constable Wruggles was making too much noise with the bullhorn.

"Now, what we want to do," Bean heard him say as they drew

closer, "is break up into groups of ten, with each group searchin' a different part of the island accordin' to the grids on this map."

"Daddy!" Ab cried.

A few people at the edge of the crowd heard the cry and, turning to see Ab and Bean running toward them at full speed, began to poke those around them and point up the street. Those closer to the front, though, were the last to know.

"Ray Lowry and Elliott Hall, you take this group to the creek side of Armburst Hill," Wruggles continued, sleeplessness showing on his face. "Viv Drew, you and Harlan Gregory take your bunch out to Lane's Island . . ."

By this time the fringes of the crowd had begun to disintegrate, and the low murmur of excitement swelled to a chorus. Mrs. Carver looked up from her worried hands and, following the eyes of the distant members of the crowd and the little sea of pointing fingers, saw Ab and Bean running toward the fire station.

"Bean!" she cried, catching Constable Wruggles in midsentence.

Within a twinkling, Mrs. Carver was being lifted off the flatbed by a couple of burly lobstermen. By the time they set her down, Bean was in her arms.

Seconds later, Ab was hoisted up on the flatbed, where she and her parents threw themselves at one another amid the tears and sobs and cheers of the crowd.

Constable Wruggles was the first to speak. "Now that this is all settled and folks can get back to breakfast, I don't s'pose you two would mind tellin' us where you've been," he studied their dirty faces and hands, "and what on earth you've been up to."

There was a general murmur of agreement, and someone lifted Bean onto the truck. As he took his place beside Ab, you could have heard a feather fall on meringue.

The kids looked at each other. Bean, who was never very comfortable in a crowd, nodded for Ab to do the talking. She cleared her throat and took a step forward.

"We found the tunnel up at the Moses Webster House. That is, we found the secret way in."

From then on, the crowd, pressing closer and closer, hung on every word as she told the whole story and hardly breathed until she was finished. Afterward there was a long silence.

"What about the treasure?" someone said at last.

"Yeah," said someone else. "Did you find anything?"

"No," said Ab. "As I said, it's just a little room, or the tunnel must have been bricked over like the other wall."

"Then all we got to do is break down the wall," suggested the first man, "and we can get a look at old Minerva's treasure."

"Let's go," said a few others, and they began to run up the street.

They hadn't gotten more than a few steps when a shotgun blast split the still morning air, sending clouds of frightened seagulls and pigeons into the sky. Everyone stopped and turned toward Constable Wruggles, who was holding a still-smoking shotgun on his lap. "Nobody's goin' nowhere," he said flatly. "What you're talkin' about is trespass, and it ain't gonna happen. That's private property."

"But the Proverbs don't own that treasure," Monty Carver objected. He was Bean's second cousin on his father's side and was just the kind of person who could be relied upon to say the kind of things that would get a crowd worked up.

Wruggles stepped to the edge of the truck and leveled a cautioning gaze at Monty. "That may be so," he said. "As I remember, that tunnel's s'posed to go to the Winthrop House. That means Maud Valliers owns half, if there is any treasure. And if there is, the courts will decide who gets what."

"It ain't theirs," Monty protested sharply. "It belongs to the whole town."

This notion found quick acceptance among many in the crowd, and Wruggles knew he'd have a riot on his hands if he didn't do something fast. "I seem to recall that your old man found a handwritten letter from Abe Lincoln to Thomas Bodwell up amongst some old company papers in your attic, didn't he?"

"So?" said Monty. He knew what was coming but couldn't think fast enough to get himself out of it.

"So, he had it sold at auction at Christy's, didn't he, down to New York City?"

Again, Monty said "So?" but with much less feeling.

"Got thirty thousand dollars, I seem to remember you tellin' me."

"Everybody knows that," said someone else. "He tells most folks down to the ferry 'fore they have had a chance to put their bags down."

Everyone laughed, especially Bean. Monty had bragged about that thirty thousand dollars as long as he'd known him.

"And he bought him a nice big lobster boat with that money, didn't he?"

Monty didn't say anything, but he seemed to shrink about two inches.

Wruggles continued: "And when he died, you come into that boat, didn't you?"

Several other people answered for Monty. "He sure did. Never had to put in a penny of his own."

"So, if we was to use your logic, we could say that letter belonged to the whole town. So I guess that means your boat belongs to the whole town."

"And so does all the money he's made lobsterin' off it," added an astute lobsterman.

"I wouldn't be surprised if that comes to a good deal more than Minerva's treasure," Wruggles continued, "whatever it is. How 'bout it?"

Monty glowered angrily at the constable, but he knew he was beaten. "You're an old fool," he spat. "And you ain't even from the island."

Bean had heard this logic before. His mother was from the mainland, though his father's family settled the island in the late 1600s.

Wruggles smiled calmly. "That's right," he said. "I'm here 'cause I choose to be, not 'cause there's no place else that'll have me."

This retort seemed to be at least as sensible as the accusation, so Monty fell silent and slunk away toward the boatyard.

"Now," said Wruggles, turning to the Proverbs, "if you want to look into this business with Maud, you go right ahead, and I hope you find a treasure and get rich and treat the whole town to a lobster dinner. But as far as real treasure goes," he put his hands on Bean's and Ab's shoulders, "I figure we've got that right here."

There was hearty applause from the crowd, which, after receiving thanks from the Petersens and Mrs. Carver, broke up.

"That took the wisdom of Solomon," said Mr. Proverb, pumping Wruggles's hand vigorously. "It could have gotten nasty."

Wruggles wrinkled his brow. "The nasty part may still be ahead," he said. "Maud Valliers likes her privacy. I don't know how she's gonna take to the idea of that tunnel. Well," he said, zipping the bullhorn into its case, "this day's turned out a lot better than it started. I'm headin' home for breakfast and a nap. Let me know what happens. Not that I'll find out long after you anyways," he added with a wink, "the way news travels 'round here."

Later that morning, after Bean and Ab had a good, long rest, they accompanied Mr. Proverb to the front door of the Winthrop House. After leaving their names, they were shown into the front hallway by the maid, known to be a French Canadian girl named Mierette whom Miss Valliers had brought from Boston.

Ab thought it funny, as she looked around, that the interior of the house looked just the way she'd imagined it would, with dark, heavily flowered wallpaper, rich oak and mahogany woodwork, fine tongue-and-groove wood floors strewn with ancient carpets, and the lower half of all the windows of ornate etched glass. It was like a place frozen in time. The maid, too, who stood waiting stiffly in her neatly pressed gray and white uniform at the foot of the stairs, accented the feeling of timelessness.

Before the Winthrop House was occupied, Bean had tried to peek in the windows. The wood louvers had always been closed, though, and had remained so even after Miss Valliers moved in, so the interior was a surprise to him. There was a heavy odor of mothballs, and everything seemed just a little past its prime. But, unlike the exterior, the inside looked clean and cared for and generally in good repair. It was a place from the past, of course, but so were about half the houses on the island.

Mr. Proverb, too, seemed lost in contemplation of his surroundings when they heard a voice and suddenly, as if from nowhere, Miss Valliers was at the top of the stairs.

"May I help you?" she said coldly. She didn't come down the stairs but stood with folded hands resting in front of her on the carved ivory head of an ebony walking stick.

At school that year, Ab had learned the word *anachronism,* and it sprang to mind as she looked at the woman amid these surroundings. She was tall and slender, about forty or so, with long, dirty-blond hair thickly braided and draped across her breast. She wore a black turtleneck and a multicolored vest covered with ornate, exotic-looking designs in gold. A black cotton skirt, which nearly touched the floor, was cinched about her waist with a broad red leather belt.

Curiously, despite her apparent great care in dressing, Miss Valliers was liberally spattered with paint from neck to knee, including her hands.

Bean saw none of that. All he noticed were the hardest, coldest eyes he'd ever seen staring down at him as if he were a dog that had tracked something nasty into the house. He checked his shoes.

Clearly she made Mr. Proverb a little uncomfortable, as well. "Ms. Valliers," he said cordially, climbing a few steps with his hand extended.

"*Miss* Valliers," the woman replied sharply. "Miss."

She made no motion toward him, so Mr. Proverb stopped and, dropping his hand, fiddled with his hat. "I'm Spencer Proverb, Miss Valliers," he continued as pleasantly as possible. "I'm sorry we haven't met yet, but you've seen my wife and me across the lane, I'm sure."

"You and your wife are of no interest to me, Mr. Proverb," Maud replied coldly. "I rarely look out my window." She glared at Bean and Ab. "There is nothing new under the sun."

"Yes, well, so," Mr. Proverb stammered unsurely. "Anyway, these children were playing in my cellar . . ."

Ab and Bean bridled a little. They hadn't been playing; they'd been investigating. But there was no point in making an issue of it.

Mr. Proverb continued, "and they came upon what seems to be the entrance to the old tunnel." He hesitated. "You've heard of the tunnel, I trust?"

"I don't listen to local gossip."

"No, no. Of course not. Not gossip at all, really. More like local legend, I'd say," Mr. Proverb explained diplomatically.

"The island is of no concern to me," Miss Valliers announced. "I have no interest in its past, present, or future. Nor do I wish to be involved with its people or their lives in any way beyond those that my needs require. I came here to get away from people and to paint. If I find my privacy compromised, I shall be on the next boat and will never look back."

"Mm. Be that as it may," Mr. Proverb plodded on doggedly, "it may interest you to know that, according to this particular legend, a great treasure is buried in the tunnel, and if so, it's—"

"You are mistaken in attempting to appeal to my sense of greed, Mr. Proverb," snapped Miss Valliers. "I am a rich woman. I have made my own fortune and have no need of another's, real or imagined. This conversation has exceeded my patience." She struck the floor sharply with her cane. "The only treasures on my property are my paintings."

She continued her lecture. "I researched this property very carefully before I purchased it. You may be sure that my boundaries extend all the way to your wall. I own the lane and everything over it and under it. If you or anyone else trespasses in any way, you shall have the law to answer to, and I will exact its full penalty without mercy. Do I make myself clear?"

Mr. Proverb, ever the gentleman, murmured some apologies and ushered Bean and Ab before him to the door.

"I will have my privacy," Miss Valliers announced in parting.

No sooner had Mr. Proverb laid his hand on the ornate bronze doorknob than a huge silhouette loomed ominously through the etched glass, and the door opened.

10

A Web of Lies

"UNCLE PHIL," Bean exclaimed in relief.

"Hey, Beans. What are you doing here? Hi, Spencer. Abenstein."

Phil's new nickname for Ab was Abenstein. She didn't have a clue what it meant, but she took it as a compliment.

"We had just come by to see Mrs. . . . ah, Mrs. . . . ah, Miss, ah . . . ," Mr. Proverb stuttered. He indicated the top of the stairs, but when all eyes turned to follow, there was no one there. Even the maid had vanished.

Uncle Phil came in and set down the portfolio cases he was carrying. He smiled. "Mm. She has that affect on people, I've noticed. A lot like Halloween here, year-round."

"She was there a second ago," said Ab.

"Oh, I don't doubt it," Phil replied. "This place is full of secret passages, and she makes use of 'em. Hardly ever uses the halls like a normal person."

Bean shuddered. "All she needs is a broomstick, if you ask me."

"Now, now, Bean. You shouldn't talk like that," Mr. Proverb admonished.

Uncle Phil laughed his big, booming, one-note laugh, and the house echoed with it. "Well, she does tend to be a little dramatic. I'll give you that. But you get so you ignore it. What's your business here, anyway?"

They all left Miss Valliers's house and walked next door, where they sat on the stone retaining wall in front of the Moses Webster House. Bean, Ab, and Mr. Proverb took turns telling the story.

"And the fire alarm went off this morning about quarter of six or so and didn't stop until everyone in town had gotten together down at the fire station," Mr. Proverb said in conclusion. "Then, just as we were about to split up into search parties, these two came strolling down the street, big as life."

Uncle Phil stared from one to the other of them for a long time. "Hmph," he said finally. "I thought when I was off the island, the whole place closed down." He paused again for a long, uncomfortable minute. "So, you found the tunnel. I never gave that old cistern a thought." He pounded Bean on the back. "Well done."

"But she won't let us down there," Ab complained. "We don't even want the treasure, but I just can't stand not knowing if it's there, and what it is."

"Well, I guess that part will just have to stay a mystery," said Mr. Proverb, slapping his knees as he stood up. "I'm sure not going to tussle with that woman in court. See you later, Phil. You two, see if you can stay out of trouble for a while, okay?" He patted Ab on the head and lumbered inside.

Bean had been thinking. "What I can't figure out is, who's been using that room, and why?"

"What do you mean?" asked Uncle Phil. "You said it was empty. So, no one's using it."

Ab followed Bean's argument. She cast a sidelong glance at Uncle Phil. "Somebody let us out," she said. "And before that, those nights I heard the breathing, that was the air that gets compressed in that little room when the floor comes up and the door is closed. Somehow the air is forced up between the walls, and it just kind of gushes out at my end of the house."

"Very good," said Bean. "That explains it, and the thumping you heard."

"Some kind of counterweights and pulley system in the wall," added Ab.

"That raises or lowers as the cisterns empty and fill." Bean finished the explanation.

"Hydraulics. Just as you said," stated Ab.

"Hydraulics," said Uncle Phil thoughtfully. "Hmph. Imagine that."

"Which still leaves us with the question of who's been using that room, and why." said Bean.

"There's another possibility," said Uncle Phil. "An old piece of machinery like that could just be going off by itself."

"How?" asked Bean.

"Well, you say there's a spring flowing into the cistern. That means there's a regulator of some kind. And that means a gasket. What if it's worn away and the water just trickles in all the time instead of when somebody wants it. When it gets full, it trips the mechanism. That would explain why Abby's heard those noises at all hours of the night."

Phil continued: "If that's the case, it's probably been going up and down for years, but nobody noticed it because all the noise was at the back of the house. That room hasn't been used much over the years.

"Well, you'll have to show it to me sometime." Phil glanced at his wrist as if he were wearing a watch, which he wasn't. "Gotta get to the boat. See you kids later." He crossed the street and climbed into his truck. "Don't go getting lost again," he said as he pulled away.

Bean and Ab watched the faded yellow truck sputter noisily down the street. It was trailing a cloud of light blue smoke.

"I don't buy it," said Ab.

"Me neither," Bean agreed. "This whole thing's fishier than a bait bag on a hot rock, and I want to know what's goin' on."

"But how can we find out? You don't still suspect Mr. Proverb, do you?"

That would have taken more imagination than even Bean had. "No, not anymore," he confessed.

"Then who else is there? The only other people in the house now are Mrs. Proverb and my mom and dad. Everyone else is gone." Bean saw the sudden flash in her eyes. "You don't think—"

"No, no," said Bean quickly. "I don't think it's your folks, or Mrs. Proverb." An idea suddenly came to him. "But I wonder . . ."

"Wonder what?"

"What if there's someone else living in the house?" He looked at her with widening eyes. "Someone nobody knows about."

A three-pronged tingle scampered up Ab's back and arms and met at the nape of her neck, where a little nest of light hairs stood quivering at attention. She grabbed Bean's arm. "Don't say that," she screamed. Then, almost instantly, she added, "What do you mean?"

Bean explained his idea. "Remember when Uncle Phil said the Winthrop House was full of secret passages? What if the Moses Webster House is, too?"

They both turned their eyes slowly toward the tower of the Moses Webster House. "And somebody's living up there," said Bean. "Someone who nobody knows about."

"Oh, Bean," said Ab, tugging frantically at his arm. "I wish you hadn't said that. It's too creepy. How am I supposed to sleep here anymore?"

"Unless . . . ," said Bean.

"Wait a second." Ab held up her hand. "Is this 'unless' for the better or for the worse? 'Cause if it's for the worse, I don't want to hear it."

Bean's gaze traveled deliberately across the lane to the Winthrop House. Ab's followed. "Unless she's already found the tunnel."

"You mean Maud Valliers is the one opening it?"

"Sure," said Bean, warming to the idea. "What if all the workings for the secret tunnel are on this side?"

"In the Moses Webster House?"

"Right. She probably doesn't even know it—or didn't—but that light you saw when we were trapped . . ."

"It could have been Maud Valliers, down in the tunnel," said Ab, her mind beginning to race. "Come to think of it, who else could it have been?"

"Which would mean that she saw our note when we pushed it through the crack," Bean theorized. "So she flipped the switch, or whatever it is, and let us out."

"You're right," said Ab. "'Til then, she probably didn't know about the hydraulics. She probably figured that all the mechanism was on her side, buried in the ground somewhere."

"I bet she's not a happy tadpole right about now," Bean theorized. "She thought she had the tunnel all to herself, but now she knows we know."

"The whole town knows," said Ab. "I bet she was just waiting for the perfect time to take the treasure off the island in some way that no one would be suspicious."

Bean and Ab secreted themselves behind a bank of beach roses, through which they could study the Winthrop House unseen. "If that's the case," Ab continued, "she'll have to start moving stuff out right away, in case people get too curious."

"Anyone we know?" Bean said with a laugh.

"How can we find out what's down there?" Ab said after a few minutes. "It's driving me crazy not knowing."

Bean shrugged. "You heard her. She owns all the property right up to Mr. Proverb's wall."

"So she says," Ab retorted. "But that doesn't make sense. I mean, it doesn't make sense that Moses Webster would have let Isaiah Winthrop own the whole tunnel, does it?"

"No, it doesn't," Bean replied after deliberating a minute. "Maybe we should check it out. Let's go see Eb Clark."

"He lives all the way up to Dyer Island, doesn't he?" said Ab, following breathlessly behind Bean as he sailed across the street, over the fence, and down the walk to his house.

"No problem," Bean called over his shoulder. He bounded onto the wood walkway and came to a stop against the railing. "We've got transportation." He gestured grandly at the moped. Despite its new coat of paint, it still inspired skepticism rather than confidence.

"You're not serious."

"Why not? Mom had Alby Oakes go all over it. See? He even got the brake lights and the blinkers working." Bean turned on the key and flipped the switches on the handlebars. Ab was suitably impressed as the corresponding equipment came to life.

"I wonder if he fixed the horn," said Bean, placing his ear in close proximity to the rusty metal disk. He pressed the button. At once a startlingly loud shriek, as if someone had stepped hard on the tail of a large mechanical cat, shattered the stillness. Bean and Ab nearly left their socks. Especially Bean, whose look of shocked amazement was fixed as if he'd been sprayed with liquid nitrogen.

"What?" he said numbly.

"I think it works," Ab observed, still holding her ears.

"Come on," said Bean after he'd shaken off the effects of the blast. He straddled the seat and pumped the starter pedal a few times, until the engine purred calmly to life. "Pile on."

"Pile on where?" said Ab, scanning the bike for any sign of a seat.

Bean patted the metal luggage rack atop the rear wheel. "Right here. Practically a sofa."

Ab overcame her better judgment and climbed on. "It's not very comfortable," she complained. "What am I supposed to hold on to?"

Bean smiled. "Me," he said, and he twisted the throttle and lifted his feet. Reflexively, she threw her arms around him as they sputtered across the grass, down the walk, and onto Main Street.

It was about three and a half miles to Dyer Island. Off the main road, there were potholes everywhere, most of which Bean managed to hit at a brisk clip. Ab groused bitterly in his ear most of the way, but deep down she was enjoying the exhilaration and freedom. Now the whole island was theirs.

They scooted down a little-used driveway of grass and bare granite ledge, then pulled to a stop near the kitchen door of a tidy little red

Cape overlooking the Reach. Off in the distance, beyond the White Islands, loomed the Camden Hills on the mainland and, to the south a mile or so, the high dome of Hurricane Island.

"My bum hurts," said Ab, stumbling off the bike and massaging the offended region vigorously. "I think you missed one of those potholes."

"I'll get it on the way back," said Bean with a chuckle. He rapped loudly at the door, which was soon opened by a balding, stoop-shouldered man who greeted them warmly. "Beanbag, Abigail. Well, well. Come in, come on in." He opened the screen door wide and stood as far to the side as his ample belly allowed. "Mother," he bellowed, even though Mrs. Clark was only fifteen feet away, at the other end of the kitchen, "we've got comp'ny. Haul out that rhubarb pie again."

Mr. Clark pulled a couple of shiny white ladderback chairs from the table and motioned Ab and Bean toward them. Seeing that Ab was about to protest, he added, "Now, now. None of that. You sit and wrap yourself around some've Ma's pie or you'll break her heart. You don't want to do that, do ya?"

As Ab sat sheepishly at the table, she cast a quick glance at Eb's substantial girth. She couldn't help but think it had been a long time since he'd broken his wife's heart.

"Well, my goodness," Mrs. Clark said as she placed two huge, steaming slices of rhubarb pie on the table. "Abigail, you've turned into quite the young lady since I saw you last."

Bean stopped himself from saying, boy, ain't that the truth only by stuffing a forkful of pie into his mouth. He mumbled appreciatively about the pie, and chewed.

Ab flushed bright crimson.

"Happens at that age," said Eb with a twinkle in his eye as he smiled at his wife. "Now, then. Much as Ma'd like to think so, I imagine it was more than her pie brought you all the way out here. What's up?"

Bean swallowed and cleared his throat. "It's about the Winthrop House."

"Why ain't I surprised?" said Eb, ladling a hefty dollop of double cream onto Ab's slice of pie, then watching each mouthful as she ate it with almost as much pleasure as if he were eating it himself. "You're the second person today's asked the same question, and I'll tell you the same as I told them. Near as I recall, Frog Hollow's split dead even between the houses."

"What's Frog Hollow?" Ab asked.

"That's the name of the lane," Eb explained.

"I didn't even know it had a name," said Bean, washing down the last of the pie with the cold milk that Mrs. Clark had placed in front of him.

"Sure it does. Every road on the island has a name," said Eb. "Used to have street signs, too. Wrought iron, mostly. Over time they just come down one after the other, and no one saw fit to replace 'em. Now only us old folks remember the names and the streets they go to."

"Who else asked?" said Ab. "About the lane—Frog Hollow?"

"Maud Valliers herself," said Eb. He cast a knowing sidelong glance at the kids. "I heard what happened down at the fire station this morning, and I'll tell you what I think." He tapped the side of his nose. "I think there's some kind of treasure down in that cellar. And," he added with emphasis, "that woman's down there right now, slidin' it all over to her side of the lane.

"'Course," he concluded, brushing crumbs from the table into his hand, "there's nothin' anyone can do about it without some kind of legal footwork. Seems the only way into the tunnel's from her side, since your side's plugged up."

Mr. Clark stood, went to the screen door, and pushed it open. "Nope. You ask me, she's down there right now, and you can bet when they finally break through—if they ever do—there won't be so much as a widow's mite on poor ol' Proverb's side. That Maud Valliers, she bears watchin'. That's what I think."

11

Trapped Again

The evening wind was picking up generous handfuls of salt-laden air and the scent of fresh-cut grass and tossing them in Ab's and Bean's faces as they puttered back toward town at twenty-five miles an hour. It felt like a hundred miles an hour except on the hills, where gravity forced them to a near standstill. Twice Ab had to climb off, because the moped simply refused to carry them both uphill.

"What now?" Ab hollered breathlessly as she ran to catch up with Bean after one such stretch. She felt him shrug as she climbed on behind him.

"You think there's really a treasure down there? I mean, really, Bean?"

Bean fell silent for a minute as they coasted down the far side of Harbor Hill to the village. "I didn't really think so at first," he allowed. "Back when we started, it was like a game—you know, somethin' to do. But once we got going, I began to wonder, what if there really is a treasure? I mean, what if all the old stories are really true? Then, when we found the hydraulics and the tunnel . . . well, that changed everything."

It sure did, Ab thought. A jumble of thoughts and feelings raced through her brain—excitement, curiosity, fear, a little apprehension—and over the whole confusing mixture loomed the glitter of gold and the ominous figure of Maud Valliers.

Instinctively she squeezed Bean with both arms. A new, mysterious feeling struck through him, as if that squeeze had somehow connected the terminals of some sleeping biological battery deep in his core. The resulting shock nearly knocked him off the bike.

Not that he'd have noticed.

"You're right," said Ab. "This is a real mystery."

Bean pulled to a stop beside the pond near his grandparents' house and shut off the engine with a flip of his thumb.

"That was fun," said Ab. She climbed off and ran her fingers through her hair, which was stiff with the potion of summer.

Bean didn't reply. He took a step or two to the edge of the pond, sat on a large rock, and stared at the still water. The wind had left them and gone to play elsewhere.

"I know what you're thinking," Ab announced.

"You do?" Bean replied, a little alarmed. That was the last thing he wanted her to know.

"Sure," said Ab lightly, plucking a piece of grass and sticking it between her teeth, the way Bean always did. "You're trying to figure out a way to get into the tunnel and find out what's going on up there."

Bean didn't take his eyes off the water. Something told him it was important not to look at Ab right now, for fear she'd be able to read his thoughts through his eyes. Everything had changed. The whole world had flipped upside down and turned itself inside out, like the reflection of the opposite shore in the mirrorlike surface of the pond. Trouble is, he was the only one who knew it. Everyone else was acting as though nothing had happened.

"A mirror," he cried, a new thought suddenly displacing the others.

Ab waited. She knew that Bean was turning over some new idea in his fertile mind. She could tell by the way his eyes were dancing blindly, as if they were trying to catch up with the picture in his mind. Good ol' Bean, she thought.

"No," he said at last. He seemed to deflate as if someone had stuck a pin in him. "That won't work."

Ab was disappointed. "What won't work?"

"I was thinking, if we could rig up a system of mirrors from the tunnel—you know . . ." It was one of those thoughts that made less sense when it was spoken than it did in his head. "Never mind," he said.

"You mean some way to see what's in the tunnel without Maud Valliers finding out?" Ab guessed.

"Something like that. How did you know?"

"Mirrors," said Ab. "It figures, doesn't it?"

"It does?"

"But I've got something better."

Ab unzipped her fanny pack and fished out her disposable camera. "All we need to do is figure out a way to get this in there."

All at once the thoughts crystallized in Bean's brain. "I've got it." He leapt on the moped and gave the pedal the one quick, sharp pump it needed to start. "Pile on."

"Where're we going?"

"Back down the hole," said Bean confidently.

Ab, who had just "piled on," put her feet down and let Bean drive off without her. He'd gone almost to Main Street before he realized she wasn't there. Instead, she was standing back by the pond with her hands on her hips and her elbows akimbo. She was looking at him as if he had lost his mind.

He drove back. "What's the matter?"

"Are you crazy?" said Ab. It was more a declarative sentence than a question. "There's no way I'm going down there again. No way."

The sparkle in his eyes was doubled by the curious curl of his mouth. "We're going to get Maud Valliers to show us where the treasure is."

"If it wasn't getting dark, I'd say you've been out in the sun too long," said Ab.

"Just trust me," said Bean.

At first Mr. Proverb just laughed, thinking that Bean was pulling his leg. Now that he knew the boy was serious, he stuttered and sputtered, trying to find the right words.

"You can't be serious, Bean," he said.

"You can't be serious," Ab echoed. It was the first time she, too, had heard the plan.

But Bean was undeterred by their skepticism. "Listen. It'll be a small fire—just a little newspaper—and since it'll be down in the hole, it can't spread. There's nothing down there that can burn. It's all dirt and rock, right?"

"Well, yes," Mr. Proverb replied hesitantly. "But why? What's the point?"

Bean smiled as he began to explain, and his smile grew as he saw his words light a spark, first in Ab's eyes then in Mr. Proverb's.

"That's brilliant," said Ab, not waiting for her partner to finish his last sentence. "Let's go for it."

"Now, now," Mr. Proverb cautioned. Already he'd broken out into a sweat. "Let's think this thing through." He scratched his head. "Granted, it seems as if it'll work—no harm'll be done—but we don't want anything to go wrong. No one must get hurt."

"No one will," Bean assured him.

"Oh?" Mr. Proverb said dubiously. "I wish I had your confidence."

"There's nothing to worry about."

"Famous last words," said Ab. She'd heard them before.

"Just newspapers, you say?" said Mr. Proverb, who seemed to be trying to convince himself.

"That's all. Just newspapers."

Mr. Proverb deliberated for about thirty seconds. "All right," he said, grabbing his flashlight. "There's a bucket overhead in the cellar stairway. We'll use water from the cistern if we have to." He turned his excited eyes to Ab. "You go station yourself outside while Bean and I start the fire." He retrieved an armload of newspapers from a brown paper bag and tucked them under his arm. "Let's hurry, before I come to my senses."

Bean found the length of pipe that he and Ab had used earlier. While Mr. Proverb shone the light into the cistern, Bean used the pipe to poke around until he found the trip lever. He gave one quick push, and instantly the water began to drain out. As it did, the antique mechanism once more ground into action. Mr. Proverb directed the beam of light at the little room at the end of the hall. They heard a gentle grating sound, then the massive stone rose silently, ominously.

"Quick," cried Bean. With Mr. Proverb on his heels, he ran to the room and waited nervously while the floor rose high enough to let him in. "Toss me some papers."

Mr. Proverb was a little more cautious. He waited until the granite stone had stopped against the ceiling. "I think I'd better do this part," he said, descending the rough steps gingerly. Once down, he shone the light around, inspecting the room he never knew he had. "Well, I'll be . . . this is amazing." He played the light over the brick wall. "That's where the tunnel is, huh?"

Bean was busy balling up pages of newspaper and piling them into a little pyramid in the middle of the floor. "That's right. Could I have a match, please?" Neither of them noticed as the door to the room swung silently shut.

Mr. Proverb rummaged through his pockets absentmindedly, searching for the safety matches he'd brought. He studied the wall. "And you say the tunnel's half mine?"

"According to Eb, it is. He should know." Bean was getting nervous. Being in that dank, little black hole again, surrounded by the thick, earthy smell of mold and dirt, he felt as though the walls were closing in. Suddenly, he didn't want to play anymore. He wanted to get out. Manfully stifling the urge to scream and run, he crumpled the last page of newspaper and held it in his hand. "Match, Mr. Proverb?"

"Then, legally, I could just knock this wall down and walk right in," Mr. Proverb speculated. Meanwhile he found a packet of matches and began tearing one out.

"But maybe she's moved all the treasure to her side," Bean reminded him. He shot a couple of quick glances at the ceiling, which he could barely make out at the remote edges of the halo of illumination from the flashlight. Was the ceiling coming toward them? He couldn't take much more of this. "If she did, you wouldn't be able to prove that any of it had ever been on your property."

"Mm," said Mr. Proverb. "I s'pose you're right." He struck the match. Nothing happened. The little daub of sulfur fell off in a clump and landed among the pile of paper. "These are old matches," he said apologetically. "Probably been through the wash more than once." Slowly, deliberately, he began to tear another match from the pack. The moment it came loose, the cellar filled with the sound of rushing water. Startled, Bean looked up. This time he wasn't imagining things. The floor was coming down.

"Quick, Mr. Proverb. Light another one," he yelled.

Mr. Proverb, suddenly panicking so much that his hands shook, struck another match. This time there was a brief spark, but it wasn't enough to light the match.

"We've gotta get out of here," Mr. Proverb cried. He bolted up the steps, but in his haste he tripped halfway up and fell, hard, knee first on the steps. Then he fell headlong at Bean's feet—unconscious.

Just then, amid the wads of crumpled paper, the smoldering dot of sulfur burst into flame. Instantly the papers were ablaze. All the while, the great stone slab descended slowly into place. Bean knew that in seconds they'd be sealed in, and the fire would use up all the oxygen faster than it could be replaced.

If Bean couldn't think of something fast, they were doomed.

12

"You'll Never Guess What I Found"

From Ab's point of view, everything was going perfectly. She had taken up her post in the maple tree that overhung the hollow and was peering through Mr. Proverb's binoculars. From this vantage point, she was able to see over the frosted lower half of the front-door windows of the Winthrop House, through the entry, and all the way down the hall to the door that led to the kitchen at the rear of the house. She could also see a little bit of the stairs to the left and the row of doors leading to various rooms to the right.

For what seemed a long time, nothing happened. Ab was just about to put down the binoculars and give her weary eyes a rub when the maid burst from the kitchen, apparently in response to some call that Ab couldn't hear. For a moment, the maid stood in the middle of the hall, gesturing wildly and apparently talking or yelling up the stairs.

In the next instant, Maud Valliers came running down the stairs and seemed to be giving hasty instructions to the distraught girl, who responded by running to the phone that sat on an ornate marble table near the parlor door. She picked it up and began dialing frantically.

"Perfect," said Ab. "Now we'll see what kind of genius you are, Bean."

She quickly refocused the binoculars on Maud, who had descended the last few steps, rounded the newel post, and was standing in front of what appeared to be a blank wall under the stairs. She looked nervous. She seemed to be waiting until her maid's back was turned.

Sure enough, as the maid bent her attention to the telephone, Maud reached up quickly and pressed a piece of molding, which must have been a switch of some sort, because a segment of the wall instantly swung away. She was through it and out of sight before Ab had time to blink.

"A secret passage!" Ab cried aloud. The hidden door closed quietly and, as it did, a little puff of smoke wafted into the hall. After a minute or so, the maid put down the receiver and, registering no alarm that her mistress had disappeared, rushed to the front door. She opened it wide and stood nervously wringing her hands and pacing back and forth. She wouldn't have to wait long, Ab knew, before Tiny Martin and the rest of the volunteer fire department would be careening up the street with lights flashing and sirens wailing. In fact, Ab could already hear them in the distance.

What was Maud up to, though? That was the question in Ab's mind. She trained her binoculars once again on the secret passage and focused just in time to see it slide open. Maud emerged carrying some large, flat objects wrapped in what looked like black plastic trash bags.

Ab bent her brows in bemusement. This was not what she'd expected. "Paintings?" she said. "She's saving her paintings?" Then she remembered Maud's words of the day before: "The only treasures on my property are my paintings." Ab watched as the woman rushed frantically through the kitchen door. She must be taking the paintings out to the barn, maybe to her car. The same routine was repeated two more times before the firemen arrived, though less than five minutes had elapsed.

Two minutes more and a crowd of townspeople had arrived. They were helping the maid carry valuables onto the front lawn for safekeeping while the firemen tracked down the source of the smoke.

Amid the confusion, Ab found it easy to carry out the next part of the plan. She slipped unnoticed into the Winthrop House and made her way along the hall, mingling with the tide of firefighters, to the hidden door. She chose her time carefully. While Maud Valliers was leading the firemen through the house, Ab pressed the molding; the panel swung open noiselessly. Quickly she plunged through it into the darkness. It took her no time to find the latch on the inside, and she closed the door behind her

She flipped on her flashlight. The smell of smoke was strong, but she couldn't see it. It must have been pushed through the tunnel and up through the walls, as Bean had predicted. Shining the light around her, Ab found herself on the landing of what appeared to be an old flight of cellar stairs. That made sense, because the stairs to the second floor were directly overhead. To the left, as she descended, was a relatively new wall of plasterboard, mudded and taped but still unpainted. Maud had it sealed off, Ab said to herself. But why?

At the bottom of the steps, on top of the rough granite floor, was a large concrete slab. In each corner of the slab was a thick bolt that had apparently been sawed off and was surrounded by a ring of rust. Something heavy had stood there once, something that was meant to stay put, but it wasn't there now.

The wall behind the little cement plateau was plastered, as it was in the little room on Mr. Proverb's side. That was unusual. Scanning the wall with the beam of her flashlight, Ab saw that it met an interior foundation wall to the right and, to the left, the new plasterboard wall, which turned at a right angle at the foot of the stairs. The cement platform was the same size and shape as the floor of the little room across the lane. "That must be the door," she said out loud, almost scaring herself with the sound of her own excited voice. "Now all I need to do is find . . ." Carefully and methodically she played the light along the walls. There had to be a switch somewhere, some little irregularity, some . . .

That's when she saw it: a rectangular notch that had been cut from the upright eight-by-eight-inch timber at the bottom of the stairs. It wasn't a feature that would normally have attracted her interest, except that the edge of the notch had been worn smooth from frequent use, and there were no spiderwebs in the dark recess, as there were everywhere else.

Slowly, she reached into the notch with her hand. She felt the sides, top, bottom, the back. Nothing. No button. No knobs. "But this must be it," she said aloud in frustration. The sound of her voice awakened her ears to the fact that the footsteps on the floor above weren't as numerous as they had been, and most of the activity was centered in the front rooms. They must have found that there was no fire, she thought to herself.

When everyone was gone, Maud might return at any time, reasoned Ab. More out of perplexity than with any rational plan, Abby poked hard at the interior surfaces of the notch. First around the bottom. Nothing. Then around the middle. Nothing. Then around the top. Bingo. The top of the back pressed in, forcing the bottom out into a kind of lever. Seconds later the great stone wall swung aside, revealing a little room and a shallow flight of stairs—the mirror image of those on the other side.

Taking the steps two at a time, with her heart riding on her shoulder, she emerged into a long, wide room with a rounded ceiling. This was clearly Maud's studio. Finished paintings were stacked against the walls, and others in various stages of completion rested on easels around the room.

Because Maud ascribed to the school of art that "required more paint than talent," as Uncle Phil had said, nearly every surface of the room was covered with dots and spots and splashes, making the space, in an odd way, a work of art in itself.

Why hadn't Maud come after these? Ab wondered.

But the room itself yielded no treasure. The only odd thing was that the room, although long, wasn't as long as Ab had imagined it would be, and the far end wasn't brick, as suggested by the wall in the room that she and Bean had found. Instead it was plaster. In fact, all the walls—which arched together to form the ceiling, as might be expected in a tunnel—were plaster. The only irregularities in them were two narrow rectangles high on either side.

"Ventilation," Ab guessed aloud. As she neared the far end of the room, she became aware of a soft hum. She used her flashlight to find its source. It was a small dehumidifier, plugged into an extension cord that ran back to a power strip beneath a long layout table.

Despite the adrenaline that still coursed through her veins, Ab felt a little disappointed.

There was no treasure. No mystery. Not even much of a tunnel, really. Just a bunch of paintings. Slowly, almost sorrowfully, she took one last look around, then made her way back toward the steps.

After listening carefully to determine that the coast was clear, she pressed the lever in the notched timber and watched the huge granite block swing silently into place. Things were now completely quiet upstairs. What if everyone had gone? How would she sneak out of the house without being seen?

These questions suddenly became irrelevant as a shaft of light appeared at the top of the stairs. Someone was coming.

Instantly, Ab switched off her flashlight and ducked through the heavy curtain of cobwebs beneath the stairs. From there she watched with unblinking eyes as feet descended. Maud's feet. It wasn't hard to recognize those paint-stained black slippers.

Maud was carrying something, apparently what she'd taken out earlier. She set down the bundle on the concrete slab, then went back up the stairs.

Ab's curiosity quickly overcame her fear. She ran around the stairs to the concrete slab, lifted an edge of the black plastic bag, and shone the light inside. She couldn't believe her eyes. Eight blank canvasses, each a different size. Each a perfect white, some held with staples, some with brads, some with tacks, others with nails. No two alike.

She didn't hear footsteps, but she heard the boards of the floor above creak. She retreated to her hiding place beneath the stairs, and together with the daddy longlegs watched as Maud brought down another bundle and laid it atop the first, then returned upstairs.

Once again, Ab looked into the bag. Once again, she was met with the puzzle of canvasses: all white, otherwise no two alike. She was quickly becoming so frustrated that she entertained the preposterous notion of stopping Maud on her next trip down, if there was a next trip, and saying, Maud, old girl, what's up with the canvasses, huh?

By the time Maud descended with another armload, Ab had pressed herself into the shadows behind the stairs. She watched with cautious interest as the artist reached into the notch in the timber, pulled down the lever, and walked through the opened wall. She was cradling the third of her bundles, which she promptly took down the stairs. Two subsequent trips followed. After the last bundle was gone and it seemed as though Maud were going to spend time in her studio, Ab cautiously abandoned the safety of her hiding place and crept up the stairs.

At the top, she flipped the latch quietly, opened the door toward her, and stepped into the front hallway.

The only sound was the maid trying to sort out the jumble of furnishings that had been placed in the parlor. Ab tiptoed past the double door just as the maid had turned her back, and she was out through the entry and into the night in a heartbeat.

"Ab," said Bean breathlessly as he ran out of the shadows across the street. For some reason, they threw their arms around each other, which Bean decided was a good idea. He could feel her heart pounding. "Are you okay?"

She drew him quietly out of the glow of the streetlight. "Bean, you'll never guess what I found."

"You'll never guess what happened to Mr. Proverb and me," said Bean, hardly listening to what she said.

"Let's go get an ice cream and talk about it up at the bandstand," Ab suggested. For Ab, ice cream was the answer to everything. It occurred to Bean that if the world was coming to an end, Ab would want to get an ice cream cone and talk about it.

On their way, Ab told Bean what had happened to her. But she didn't tell him about the white canvasses. She would save that for later.

Once they were settled, Bean began to tell his story.

13

Too Much Trouble

"ANYWAY," SAID BEAN, wiping the ice cream from his mouth with the back of his hand, then wiping it on his pants, which Ab tried to ignore, "there we were, with the floor almost all the way down and Mr. Proverb passed out—just lyin' there—and smoke so thick we couldn't hardly see nothin'."

Ab was too eager to hear the rest of the story to correct her companion's English.

"And I must've been leanin' against the wall, or somethin', 'cause all of a sudden I felt this loose brick. I couldn't get my fingers into the cracks anywhere, so I just hit it as hard as I could." He held out his bloody knuckles for her inspection and, when she had shown the required amount of sympathy and he had said, "Aw, it don't hurt much," he continued. "Anyway, one end of the brick swung out just in time to stop the slab. I mean, if I'd been half a second slower, even an eighth of a second—"

"I get the picture," Ab cut him off. She didn't need any more drama in her life at the moment. "Then what?"

"Well, I took off my shirt and smothered the fire with it, but it was mostly out already. That newspaper burns some ol' fast, and the smoke was gone in no time. As I said, the slab comin' down forced the smoke through the tunnel and into the walls on Maud's side."

"What happened to poor Mr. Proverb?" asked Ab. She had finished her sugar cone and was dabbing daintily at the corners of her mouth with the soggy napkin.

"He came to after a second, groanin' and holdin' his head and his knee. But as soon as he remembered where he was, he was on his feet, howlin' out that crack between the slab and the floor—where the brick was—but 'course the door was closed, so it didn't do any good."

"But how did you get out?"

"That's the funny thing. I figured we'd just have to sit tight 'til you come to find us, but all of a sudden the water started rushin' and the slab started to rise all by itself."

"Not all by itself," said Ab. "I bet that's when Maud came down and started collecting those bags I told you about."

A light went on in Bean's eyes. "So that's what happened. She tripped it on her side."

"Just the way she did when you and I were trapped down there."

"You mean, she didn't find the note?"

"I don't see how she could have," said Ab, vividly recalling Maud's studio. "There wasn't anyplace for it to come through."

"But it went somewhere," said Bean, perplexed.

Ab thought of something. "You say you took a brick out of the wall. What was behind it?"

"Behind what?" said Bean. "The brick?"

"Don't tell me," said Ab, holding up her hand. "I already know. It was plaster."

Bean reflected thoughtfully. "No," he said. "I mean, it was hard to see with the smoke and all, but I'd say there wasn't anything there. Just space. The tunnel, I guess."

Ab's eyebrows knit in confusion. "That can't be," she said. "I saw the end of the tunnel myself. It was plastered on Maud's side."

"Well, that's easy enough to check out," said Bean. "All we have to do is go look at the place where I took out the brick. But let's go to my house first. We need a decent flashlight."

When they arrived at Bean's house, they were surprised to find Mr. and Mrs. Proverb and Ab's mom and dad there. They could see them through the kitchen window, sitting around the table, talking earnestly with Mrs. Carver.

"Uh-oh," said Ab. "This doesn't look so good."

Bean agreed.

Tentatively, they opened the back door and walked into the entryway. Instantly all conversation ceased. They opened the door to the kitchen, which wasn't usually closed at this time of year, and stepped into the room.

The looks they got from the adults made the room seem smaller than it was.

"Hi," said Bean as casually as possible. "What's up?"

"Hi, kids," said Mrs. Carver. Her hands were folded tightly in front of her on the table, and her face seemed flushed and tense. "Come on in and take a seat." Ab started to close the door behind her. "You can leave that open," said Mrs. Carver. "It's a little warm in here."

Bean and Ab sat down in the big, squeaky wood rocking chairs by the two windows. They looked apprehensively at each other, then at their elders.

Mr. Petersen turned to Mrs. Carver. "Do you want to tell them, or should I?"

"I will," said Mrs. Carver, sitting up stiffly. Her hands were still folded and unmoving, but her knuckles were white. As she looked at Ab and Bean, her eyes softened. "You guys have really put us through the wringer lately."

"What do you mean?" said Ab innocently.

"I mean, it was one thing when the two of you were running around pretending one thing or another."

"Nobody got hurt," said Mrs. Petersen, anxiety evident in her eyes.

"That's right," said Mrs. Carver. "Nobody got hurt. But lately things have gotten out of hand."

"But—" Bean began to protest, but Mrs. Carver held up her hand.

"I know. I encouraged you," she said. "I shouldn't have. I didn't realize how really dangerous things had gotten."

"And I'm to blame, too," said Mr. Proverb. "I got all caught up in the thing, like a darn fool." Mrs. Proverb patted him on the shoulder. "And I can't say you should know better, when I should have known better myself. All this," he indicated the bandage on his head and his hurt knee, "is my own fault. I just want you to know that neither of you are to blame for what I brought on myself. But when I think what could have happened to you, Bean . . . Well, it won't happen again. I'm going to see to that."

"But, Mom," Bean interjected. "I think one more trip down the tunnel and we'll be able to figure it out. You know the brick I took out of the wall. . . ?"

Mr. Petersen shook his head, raised his eyebrows, and looked beseechingly at Mrs. Carver.

"No, Bean," said his mom. " There won't be any more trips to the cellar. We've had two near misses already, and I think Mr. Petersen's right. The whole town has been turned inside out in one way or another because of you two. Next thing we know, they'll be storming up the walk with torches in their hands, like the villagers in a horror movie." She stopped and smiled at them. "Well, before it comes to that, we've decided . . . that is . . ." She hesitated.

Mr. Petersen took over. "We've decided that you and Ab shouldn't spend time together anymore."

Ab was on her feet instantly. "But Dad!" she protested. She couldn't believe what she was hearing.

"Listen to your father," said Mrs. Petersen sharply. Clearly, recent events had taken their toll on her emotionally. Her eyes, usually warm and sparkling, looked haunted and tired. Only now did Ab begin to appreciate what she'd put her mother through. Suddenly, she was sorry.

"It's time you two went your separate ways," said Mr. Petersen.

Bean flashed a desperate look of appeal at his mother, who averted her eyes. She'd never done that before. Mr. Petersen was clearly in control. Now more than ever, Bean wished his dad was home.

Mr. Petersen continued. "I think you've both got too much imagination for your own good." He attempted a smile. "And you just kind of feed on each other, until you've lost all common sense. Before you know it," he snapped his fingers, "you're in over your heads. It's bad enough to endanger yourselves, but now your games have endangered others and are causing no end of trouble."

"The idea of starting a fire," Mrs. Petersen exclaimed. "Why, I can't imagine what ever—"

Mr. Petersen held up his hand, and she fell silent. "Please, Jill, we've been over that. The point is," he said, turning again to the kids, "it just won't do. So we think it's best if the two of you don't spend any time alone together."

Bean rose again in protest, but once more Mr. Petersen held up his hand in a way that Bean knew meant no further discussion.

"You can still go with the rest of the kids and get ice cream or go for boat rides with the others, but no more motorcycle rides."

"Moped," Bean corrected softly, but his mother gave him a look that let him know that further comment would not be welcome.

"At least for a while," said Mrs. Carver, trying to dull the sharp edge of the injunction.

Mr. Petersen picked up his floppy old Irish walking hat. "Well, I don't know about that. Maybe it's time the kids found themselves some new friends. We'll see. Come along, Abigail."

Abby rose from the chair as if in a trance and cast a forlorn gaze at Bean. Did she imagine there were tears in his eyes? Shock and disbelief, anyway.

"You understand, Bean," said Mr. Petersen as he ushered his family to the door, "we don't have anything against you personally. It's just that you and Ab, who are great kids separately, just seem to lose all judgment when you're together. So, before anything really disastrous happens . . ." He didn't finish the sentence but looked around the room, first at Mrs. Carver, who was still looking away, then at Mr. and Mrs. Proverb, who had also risen to leave. "Well, we have to take steps. I'm sure, in time, you'll understand." He put on his hat. "Goodnight. I'm sorry it had to turn out this way."

He nodded toward Bean's mom. "Mrs. Carver," he said softly.

Ab and Bean locked eyes once more as she stumbled to the door. She tried to say something, but there were no words to describe the sinking, sick feeling she felt inside.

Bean didn't know what to do. He looked at his mom, who, for once, seemed as helpless as he. The slamming of the screen door awakened him to the enormity of what had just happened.

"Mom," he said, his voice as weak as if he'd had the wind knocked out of him, "me and Ab aren't bad."

"I know that," said Mrs. Carver warmly. "So do Ab's mom and dad. It's just that they're worried about Ab."

"I know, but it's—"

It was Mrs. Carver's turn to hold up her hand. "I can understand how they feel, Bean. Mr. Proverb explained how dangerous that old contraption is, how you nearly got trapped in there, not to mention starting the fire. What if Maud had a heart attack thinking that her house was on fire?"

Bean hadn't thought of that.

"Or Mr. Proverb, for that matter. He's not a young man anymore."

Bean hadn't thought of that, either.

"Mr. Proverb said you told him that nothing could go wrong," Mrs. Carver continued. She sat down across the table from him. "That's not something you'll say when you're a little older and have had more experience. Things can always go wrong, and one little mistake or error in judgment, like tonight, could end up with someone getting badly hurt. Or worse."

Bean caught the emphasis and finally understood that his and Ab's actions didn't affect just them but a lot of other people as well. All this had obviously not been easy on his mom, either. And he'd promised his dad he'd take care of her. He hung his head. "I'm sorry, Mom," he said at last, and meant it.

Mrs. Carver smiled. "That's a good sign. If you'd argued or tried to make excuses, I'd have known you weren't as mature or responsible as I'd hoped."

Bean smiled weakly. "Does that mean I can see Ab now?"

"I'm afraid not," his mom said sadly. "Maybe someday her folks will give you guys another chance. Meanwhile, think before you act. Okay?"

"Okay," said Bean quietly.

"And you're not to go down in Mr. Proverb's cellar again."

Bean shook his head. Somehow, without Ab, it didn't matter anymore. "No, ma'am."

"Good. That poor man's scared to death of a lawsuit."

Mrs. Carver stood up, came to Bean's side, and, taking his chin in her hand, tilted his head until he was looking up in her face. "I don't care if there's fifty million dollars in that tunnel," she said, her eyes damp and serious. "Nothing is worth losing you. You hear?"

Again Bean nodded. He reached up and put his arms around her neck and patted her reassuringly on the back, just the way his dad did when he was around. "Okay, Mom," he whispered. "Okay."

That night in bed, as Bean stared at the old familiar cracks in the ceiling, he wrestled with about a hundred different thoughts, but two in particular kept bobbing to the surface. First, how was he going to face the rest of the summer without Ab? He'd just left her less than an hour ago, and already there was a rotten, hollow feeling somewhere between his heart and his stomach that wouldn't go away, no matter which way he turned. Even praying didn't help much. He couldn't concentrate on the words. Second, they were so close to unraveling the mystery. If only he could get into the little room one more time.

Finally, he couldn't take it anymore. He crept out of bed and slipped on his clothes, then he squeezed through the back window, dropped onto the shed roof, and slid down the oil tank and onto the ground.

The night was cool and foggy and the air so sweet and pungent he could almost chew it. Must be low tide, Bean deduced. The grass was tall and wet, so his canvas sneakers were soaked through long before he reached the sidewalk.

The air was still. The town was asleep. The only sound was the foghorn off Greens Island and the heavy drops splattering from the tips of the leaves.

For a long time he just walked. He needed to clear his head and collect his thoughts. Before long, though, his feet had carried him to the far end of Frog Hollow. Becoming aware of his surroundings, he raised his eyes and cast a hopeful gaze at the back of the Moses Webster House. It was dark except for one warm rectangle of light that hung like a window in the fog.

Ab's room. Like him, she was awake. He walked on in silence.

14

Something Spooky

AB'S PARENTS KEPT HER SO BUSY WITH BOAT RIDES, picnics, sailing lessons, and swimming that she and Bean didn't get so much as a glimpse of each other for a whole week. So it was with a nervous feeling in his throat that Bean headed out the back door and across the street to the bandstand for Uncle Phil's ride to get ice cream. Would Ab be there? If she was, how was he supposed to behave toward her? What would they talk about?

The back of Uncle Phil's truck was already filled with kids, laughing, pushing, and debating at high volume about what kind of ice cream was best. But Ab wasn't among them. Phil was leaning out the window of the cab. "Comin', Beans?"

Bean wasn't sure. Nothing was the same without Ab. Even ice cream. "No," he said as Phil started the engine. "I guess not."

Phil shrugged. "Suit yourself." He placed his chin in the crook of the arm that rested on the window. "Too bad about Ab."

It was Bean's turn to shrug. That's all he could do.

"Well," said Phil stoically. "Maybe next week?"

"Maybe," said Bean.

He stood watching as the truck drove away. Some of the kids called and waved for him to jump aboard, but he just stuck his hands in his pockets and turned away, full of feelings he didn't know what to do with.

A big chunk of tar had broken off the pavement, and he began to kick it absentmindedly, every now and then glancing down the road at the Moses Webster House. It was easy to imagine Ab running up the street toward him, her hair bouncing all over the place and the peel of laughter that always seemed to precede her cry of "Hey, Beanbag."

But it was just his imagination. The street was empty except for two people he didn't recognize who were walking arm in arm toward the church. He glanced at them idly as he wandered over to the galamander, which stood nearby. A relic of the island's quarrying days, the galamander was a massive oak and iron wagon with nine-foot rear wheels. It had once been used to carry slabs of granite from the quarries to the cutting sheds. There were pictures of it up at the Historical Society, showing it being pulled through town by a team of twelve rugged oxen. Since then, the galamander had been set up as a memorial to the industry—long since gone—and had doubled as a kind of jungle gym for generations of island kids.

For the first time Bean noticed that the church parking lot was full of cars. "What's going on there?" he said to himself. Then he remembered: a chowder supper. His mother had steamed a bucket of mussels and taken them up earlier. If there was one thing Bean liked more than ice cream, it was a chowder supper. But he hadn't felt much like eating all week, and he didn't now either. For a few moments he stood deliberating.

About this time his attention was again drawn to the couple walking up the street, who were now close enough that he could distinguish their features. Although he recognized them individually, it was almost impossible to imagine two more unlikely people together: Maud Vallier's maid, Mierette, and his cousin Monty. Monty was dressed up in his Sunday best and—Bean hated to admit—looked quite handsome and dashing, in an awkward sort of way. He'd apparently been practicing his small talk, too, because Mierette was giggling delightedly at whatever he was saying.

Bean didn't want to talk to Monty, so he ducked behind the galamander. It soon became evident that this evasive maneuver was unnecessary, however, because Monty and Mierette seemed to be so wrapped up in each other that if King Kong had been lying dead in the road, they may well have walked over him without noticing.

As the couple passed, Bean shook his head in disbelief. But his mind was made up: He was going to the chowder supper. There was something unsettling about that pairing, something he couldn't quite put a name on, so he was going to keep an eye on his cousin. If that meant he had to eat chowder for supper, all the better.

The vestry was crowded with islanders and summer people, as it always was for one of these traditional island dinners. Bean paid Linda Philbrook at the door, then stood in line with his plate. His mind was almost taken off his surveillance by the smell of the food.

He took a few deep, heady breaths, so thick with the aroma of lobster, clams, chowder, baked potatoes, mussels, and corn on the cob that he felt he could almost put salt and pepper on it and dig in. His appetite was back.

But just as quickly as it had come, it was gone again.

Ab and her parents were sitting at a long table in the dining room of the church vestry. Panic set in when a quick scan of the remaining tables made it evident that the only free seat in the place was between Mr. Petersen and Matilda Ames, a large, overly friendly, and talkative lady who, for as long as Bean could remember, had greeted him by pinching his cheeks and saying for all the world to hear: "Look at this handsome little man. Looks more like his dad every day, 'cept they should call him Beanpole instead of Beanbag. He's so skinny."

By the time this realization hit home, Bean had already gone mechanically through the line and was standing in the middle of the room with a full plate. Everyone else was seated, with heaping mounds of food in front of them. Somebody clinked their glass with a spoon. "Ladies and gentlemen, Reverend Candidge will say grace," announced Emily Lazaro. "Pastor?"

All heads bowed, including Bean's, but as the prayer went on—apparently Reverend Candidge had a lot to be thankful for—Bean, standing by himself in the middle of the room, pried one eye open and directed it at Ab. He nearly choked when he saw her doing the same at him. With cautious glances at her parents, she motioned him to the empty seat. He shook his head furiously, but she furrowed her brows and repeated the motion, which was not so much an invitation as a direction.

"And finally, Lord, we thank you for your bountiful provision, and the care you take of each of us, day in and day out. Be with those we love who are unable to be with us tonight, and for those who are sick, lonely, hungry, and friendless the world over, make us ever mindful and use us to be a help. In Christ's name. Amen."

By the time everybody said "amen," Bean was seated. Mr. Petersen, who opened his eyes to find the seat thus occupied, scowled reflexively but, with an effort, forced a smile. "Hello, Bean," he said. "Glad you could join us. Would you like some bread?" He handed Bean the basket of homemade bread and rolls, and Bean helped himself.

"Thanks," said Bean. He didn't know whether or not to add "sir" but finally decided it might be a good idea. "Sir."

Out of the corner of his eye, he saw Ab smile.

After a few seconds of awkward courtesies, the adults resumed their conversation. Bean cleaned his plate not so much from hunger as nervousness. All his favorite foods might just as well have been sawdust.

Now and then his and Ab's eyes would meet, but it seemed whenever they did, Mrs. Petersen would suddenly clear her throat to get Ab's attention, then shake her head almost imperceptibly.

"I'm going to get some dessert," said Ab at last. "Bean, would you like to come with me? I bet there's some strawberry rhubarb pie."

The adult conversation suddenly fell silent, and for a second it seemed as though Mrs. Petersen were going to protest, but Mr. Petersen shook his head and flicked a restraining hand at her. She settled back in her chair, and Mr. Proverb quickly began talking about how the weather was hotter in Phoenix than Atlanta but not nearly as humid.

Ab and Bean arrived at the dessert table just as a wave of small children made off with their first helpings. "It all looks so good," said Ab, taking a plate from the stack at the end of the table. She handed one to Bean, too. "What are you going to have?"

Bean felt like saying, a heart attack if you don't stop talking about food, but he didn't. If this was some kind of game Ab had to play, he'd play it, too. "I don't know," he said, scanning the table blindly. Normally, the pies, cakes, and heaping mounds of cookies, fruit, fudge, and after dinner candies would have commanded his complete attention, but now they might as well have been porcelain sculptures. "I think the lemon meringue," he decided finally. He didn't even like lemon meringue, but for some reason it seemed more grown-up than what he really wanted, which was Milly Sorenson's banana cream pie. Ab cut him a big piece of lemon meringue pie and put it on his plate.

"There you go," she said. She cut herself a piece of chocolate pudding pie and ladled on some whipped cream.

"You didn't go for ice cream tonight," she observed.

"Didn't want to."

Ab nodded. There was a little stage at the back of the room. "Want to sit over there and eat?"

Bean shot a wary glance at Mrs. Petersen, who, though trying to be discreet about it, was watching them carefully. "Don't you think they'll mind?"

Ab followed his gaze. "Oh, well, they said we could still see each other at social occasions. It's all right. Come on."

They sat on the edge of the stage. While Ab ate, Bean poked holes in the meringue with his fork.

"I love graham cracker crust," said Ab. Bean looked up from his uneaten pie. Ab's mouth was covered with chocolate, and he laughed spontaneously.

"What?" said Ab.

Bean was trying to control his laughter but still couldn't speak.

"What?" said Ab again. She started laughing, too, though she didn't know why. "What's so funny?"

"You," said Bean finally. "You have chocolate all over your mouth."

Ab suddenly stopped laughing. "No, I don't," she said, mortified. She wiped her mouth with her napkin and, to her horror, a good spoonful of chocolate appeared amid its white folds. "You didn't tell me."

"I didn't notice 'til just now," Bean said with a chuckle. "Besides, nobody else saw. There's just us two here."

It was one of those times when Bean didn't know if Ab was going to laugh or cry or get mad. For a few seconds it looked as though it could go any which way. He was relieved, therefore, when her face finally broke into a wide grin. "Do I have anything on my teeth?" she said, flashing her pearly whites.

They laughed hard for a minute or two. It seemed as though all the other people in the room just melted away.

"How've you been?" said Ab.

Bean nodded his head a little sideways.

"Miserable?" she asked.

That pretty much summed it up. And he didn't care who knew. "Yeah. Miserable."

"Me, too." Not so miserable that she didn't enjoy her pie, though, Bean noticed. "Seems as if we've been going a hundred miles an hour all week. My folks must be exhausted. I sure am."

A nearby giggle caught Bean's attention. He looked up, and Ab followed his eyes. "What is it?"

"Monty and that maid."

"Huh?"

"Maud Vallier's maid, Mierette."

"Mierette?" asked Ab. Then she saw what Bean was talking about. "She's with Monty?"

Bean nodded. "That's why I came here tonight, to keep an eye on them."

"Why?"

"'Cause somethin's not right."

"Strange couple, I'd say," Ab agreed. "But I guess she can go out with anyone she wants. She's grown up."

Bean thought a minute. He wasn't satisfied. "Nope. It doesn't figure. Him just takin' up with her like that, just now after all that's happened."

"Mm," said Ab. "Well, how do you know? Maybe she took up with him."

"That's just what I know didn't happen," said Bean confidently. "Mierette hardly ever goes out of that house, much less to the waterfront or the pool hall, which are the only places Monty ever hangs out. Nope. I'll bet you he went way out of his way to get cozy with her. The question is, why?"

It didn't seem as odd to Ab as it apparently did to Bean. "Well, she's awfully pretty. I could see why anyone would like her. And she seems nice. Just 'cause she works for Maud Valliers doesn't make her a bad person, you know. She must get awfully lonely."

"I didn't know any girl could get so lonely she'd go out with Monty," Bean said. "Besides, it's not her I'm worried about. It's him. I wouldn't trust him as far as I could throw him."

"What do you care, anyway?"

"I think he wants her to help him get the treasure," said Bean. The thought had only just crystallized in his mind before it was out of his mouth. "That's what it's all about. He's goin' to use her to get the treasure."

"You mean you think he doesn't really like her?"

"There's only room for one love in Monty's life," Bean judged. "And that's himself. No sir. That's what he's up to."

"That's despicable."

"That's Monty."

"What are we going to do about it?" said Ab.

"I don't know," Bean replied. "I don't see how we can do much of anything. Not together, anyway." He paused a moment. "There's got to be some way to get that treasure before he does."

Ab raised her eyes but not her head. "Bean?"

"Mm."

"There isn't any treasure."

"What do you mean?"

"Remember I told you I was in the tunnel? There was nothing there. Just half-finished paintings all over the place. That's all."

"But it was in the bags. The ones you said Maud rescued from the fire," Bean protested.

Ab shook her head slowly. "I looked in the bags. Empty canvasses, that's all that was in there."

"Empty canvasses?"

Ab nodded.

"In all the bags?"

Ab nodded again.

"That's all?"

"That's all."

In the silence that followed, Abby thought Bean was struggling to come to terms with reality. When he spoke, however, his words dispelled that notion.

"That makes no sense at all."

"What doesn't?"

"Why would she rescue blank canvasses and not the ones she'd already painted on?" said Bean.

"I don't know," Ab replied. "Maybe she was in shock."

"Did she seem to be in shock?"

Ab didn't have to think about that. "No. She seemed to know exactly what she was doing."

"Then why was she saving the blank ones?" Bean repeated.

Abby didn't have an answer. "I don't know."

Bean didn't know either. But he knew that it didn't add up. He was about to say so when a skinny, freckled, red-headed kid came up to them balancing a plate full of desserts. "Hey, 'bag," he said. "Is that all the dessert you got?"

"Hi, Spook," Bean replied slowly. "Looks as if you got a little of everything."

"Yup. Some ol' good. How 'bout you, Ab?"

"I had some chocolate pie."

Spooky Martin wasn't spooky at all. He got the nickname from some old song his mother and father liked. In fact, Spooky was about the most immediately pleasant person Ab had ever known. His pale blue eyes were always warm and friendly, and when he smiled, she automatically found herself smiling back. If she was in a bad mood, she soon forgot why. And his copper-red hair made him stand out half a mile away on a sunny day.

"What you guys talkin' 'bout?" Spooky asked as he pulled up the piano stool, spun it around a few times, and sat down. He noticed the quick glances that Bean and Ab exchanged in response to his question. "I bet it's the treasure, ain't it?" he speculated. When this comment got him even more silence, he knew he'd hit the nail on the head.

"There isn't any treasure," Ab said a little weakly.

"Sure there isn't," said Spooky with a wink. "Well, you don't have to tell me if you don't want to, but it'll be all over town before too long anyway."

"She's tellin' you the truth, Spook," said Bean. "That's what she was just tellin' me. She got down there in the tunnel, and there wasn't nothing—"

"Anything there," Ab corrected him and completed the sentence.

"What'd you see?" Spooky asked, his cheeks bulging with blueberry pie.

Ab told him the whole story. It was impossible to keep anything from those guileless, interested eyes. She finished about the same time he finished his dessert.

"Dang," he said. He seemed to be thinking a mile a minute. "You guys are lucky to be alive."

There's no denying that, thought Ab. Still, it was hard to be happy, considering that their investigation had been brought to a halt just when things were really getting interesting.

"I know what," said Spooky. "What if I spy for ya?"

"What do you mean?" said Bean and Ab together.

"Well, I don't claim to be no genius detective, but I got eyes. I can hang around, you know. Carry messages back and forth. That kinda stuff. It'd be fun."

Of course it occurred instantly to both Bean and Ab that their parents wouldn't be thrilled with this arrangement, but they forced that thought to the back of their minds and leaped at the suggestion.

"That'd be perfect," said Bean.

"Could you do it?" asked Ab. "I mean, would you really want to? It could be dangerous. You know what almost happened to us."

"I know," said Spooky, who apparently wasn't listening carefully. "Here's what we can do. I'll sneak down in the basement—"

"How will you get down there?" Bean interrupted.

"Easy. Through the window where they toss the wood."

"Will you fit?" Ab asked.

"Sure. Who do you think tosses all that wood every fall? And when I'm through tossin', I just crawl through the window and start stackin'. That way I don't have to track gunk through the house."

Bean was elated. Ab was not. "I don't like it, Spook. As my dad says, everyone's just been lucky so far. You could get hurt down there."

Spooky licked his plate thoughtfully. When he raised his face, the end of his nose was blue with a smattering of whipped cream. "What do you need down there? Just for me to look through the hole where the brick was, right? So? One of you guys stays outside the window, and if I have any problems, you can go get help. Okay?"

Bean was willing to agree that instant, but he hesitated for Ab's benefit.

"Shouldn't take more than a few seconds, should it?" Spooky prodded innocently. "Piece a cake."

After deliberating briefly, Ab was sold. Bean could see it in her eyes. "All right," he said, just as the words were forming on her mouth.

"How do you know it's all right?" Ab snapped indignantly.

"I know you too well, I guess," Bean said with his most disarming smile.

"When?" said Spooky, anxious to get on with things.

Bean looked around at the packed vestry. If tradition held true, there would be a community sing-along after dinner, and that could last an hour or more. "There'll never be a better time than now," he said.

"I know," agreed Ab. "You guys go do it, and I can stay here. That way nobody'll suspect anything."

"Good," said Bean. "Come on, Spook." He grabbed Spooky's arm and nearly dragged him to the table, where Bean said a quick good-bye to Mr. and Mrs. Petersen and the Proverbs.

Just as he was about to leave, Matilda Ames slapped one of her hamlike arms around his waist and gave him a squeeze. "Just you look at this handsome young man. I swear, he looks more like his dad every day, don't he?" She leaned toward him as if to address the following sentence to him, but she said it loud enough for anyone within walking distance of town to hear: "'cept I still say they should call you Beanpole instead of Beanbag. You're so skinny." She laughed heartily at her own humor, then let him go.

Seconds later, the boys were outside and Spooky was rummaging through the glove compartment of his dad's truck. "Here it is," he said, producing a big flashlight.

Forsaking the road, they dodged through bushes and backyards to the lonely end of Frog Hollow. From there they made their way to the high stone wall surrounding the big backyard of the Moses Webster property. Pressing themselves into the cover of hedges that grew against the wall, they sneaked up to the ground-level window overlooking the white-walled basement room.

"You stay here," Spooky directed. "I'll go 'round to the wood window and slide in when I'm sure nobody's comin'."

Bean tucked himself safely out of sight and waited. Through the leaves, he could see the Frog Hollow side of the Winthrop House and a good part of the street out front as well. If anyone was coming, he'd know in plenty of time to warn Spooky.

15

Sinister Deeds

"That wasn't so hard," said Spooky as he came up behind Bean and tapped him on the shoulder.

Bean nearly cleared his skin. "Spooky! You scared me half to death. What are you doin' here? Couldn't you get in?"

"Got in," said Spooky calmly.

"Got in? What do you mean, 'got in'?" said Bean. "You mean you actually got in?"

"Yup. I went up to the little room, as you said, and it was all open. I could see right down in."

"The floor was up?"

"Yup. They got it propped with a whole bunch've two-by-fours."

"So you didn't even have to open it," said Bean, a little disappointed. Flipping the jigger in the cistern, hearing the rush of the water, and watching the great slab rise was the exciting part.

"Nope," Spooky replied. "And somethin' else."

"What?"

"It looks as if they're plannin' on fillin' it in. There's about fifty bags full of concrete outside the wood window with Ted Maddox's cement mixer."

No sooner were the words out of his mouth than Bean's heart doubled its beat. That's what Mr. Proverb meant when he said he was going to do something to make sure no one got hurt down there.

"We gotta move fast," Bean said. "Did you see the hole where I took the brick out? What'd you find?"

"I found it, just where you said." Spooky held up his hand. "Even got the brick. You want it?"

"Put that down," Bean said impatiently. Spooky laughed and tossed the brick under the porch. "What'd you see?" pressed Bean.

"Dark, is all," said Spooky. "I even found this piece of pipe—I bet it's the same one you used—and I stuck it in as far as I could. It didn't hit no wall."

"I knew it," Bean exclaimed excitedly. "I figure the tunnel was divided with a wall," he picked up a pebble and threw it at a tuft of grass about halfway across the hollow, "just about there. That would be the wall Ab saw. Covered with plaster. So between there and here there's another whole section of the tunnel. That's where you stuck the pipe in and didn't feel anything."

"I didn't say I didn't feel anything," said Spooky enigmatically.

Bean objected. "Yes, you did. You said—"

"I said I didn't feel a wall."

"You felt somethin'?"

"Somethin'."

"What?"

"I dunno. But I knocked somethin' over with the end of the pipe. I heard it fall," Spooky explained.

"That's weird," said Bean.

"Not half as weird as what I didn't tell ya," Spooky replied with an air of mystery.

"What?"

"It cried," said Spooky.

Bean stared holes into his companion. "What?"

"Cried. I thought it was a cat at first. That's how it sounded—like a cat crying, you know?"

"Maybe it was," Bean conjectured.

Spooky shook his head. "Nope. Whatever it was, it thudded when it fell. Thudded and rolled a foot or so."

"Rolled?"

"Besides, from the smell of the air outta there, I'd say it's sealed up pretty tight. I don't think any cat could get in."

Remembering the whiff of stale air he'd gotten when he removed the brick, Bean agreed. "Then what was it?"

Spooky shrugged his shoulders. "Whatever it is, pretty soon it's gonna be sealed in forever."

"Unless . . . ," said Bean.

"Unless what?"

Further speculation was postponed when, preceded by a soft giggle, Mierette and Monty entered the boys' frame of reference, walking hand in hand down the street toward the Winthrop House.

"They're back early," Spooky observed.

"Stranger than a two-headed haddock, those two," Bean observed.

The boys watched for a while as Monty escorted Mierette to the door. It seemed as though they stood there forever. Bean's legs were shaking, and his back was getting tired from stooping over. "What the heck are they talkin' about all this time?" he said.

"I think he's workin' up to kiss her," Spooky theorized.

"I hope she's careful," said Bean. "She kisses him, she might lose her lips."

Apparently the thought of Mierette walking around without lips struck Spooky as so funny that, before he knew what he was doing, he laughed out loud. Instantly Monty stopped talking and looked in their direction.

"Shh," said Bean, seizing Spooky's arm in a steel grip. "Hold still," he whispered sharply.

For what seemed like many minutes, as Monty squinted to see into the shadows, Bean and Spooky sat motionless, barely daring to breathe. Relief came at last from an unexpected quarter. "Eet ees notting, jos' de cat," said Mierette, poking Monty playfully on the arm. "Come, come. You were telling me how wonderful my eyes."

"Oh, brother," said Bean under his breath as Monty resumed romancing the young girl. "Tell me how pretty my eyes," he mimicked, batting his eyelids at Spooky, who almost laughed again. This time Bean saw what was coming and slapped his hand over his friend's mouth. "Quiet," he commanded in a whisper, but he was almost laughing himself.

Traffic was beginning to pick up, indicating that the festivities had ended at the church. The activity seemed to break Monty's romantic mood. With a few words, he said his good-byes and made his way to the fence while Mierette stood on the steps, her hand on the doorknob.

"And don't forget," said Monty, looking furtively up and down the street, as if to be sure he wouldn't be overheard, "twelve o'clock tonight."

Mierette giggled and nodded, then slipped quietly into the house. Monty smiled a self-satisfied smile that Bean didn't like the look of at all and walked down the sidewalk toward Main Street.

"What's he up to?" said Bean as he crawled from the bushes, checking first to see that no one was watching from the windows of the house across the street. He gave Spooky a hand out, and they brushed themselves off.

"She's some ol' pretty," Spooky observed, adopting Ab's way of thinking, which annoyed Bean.

"Pretty's got nothin' to do with it, take my word. He's up to somethin'."

Not wishing to run into Ab and her parents on their way home from the supper, the boys took the long way down the hollow and around by the old ball field to the north end of Main Street. Most of the way they were silent, each trying to make sense of things in their own way.

"What was all that about midnight, do ya think?" said Spooky as they emerged onto the blacktop.

That was the same thing Bean had been thinking about. "I don't know," he said, his eyes brightening, "but I know how to find out."

Spooky was curious. "How?"

"If you wanna find out what your mother's cookin' for supper, you go into the kitchen," Bean philosophized.

Spooky got the message. "And if you want to find out what's goin' on with Mierette and Monty at twelve o'clock, you watch 'em."

"Bingo."

"So we sleep out in the tree house tonight?"

"Bingo again," said Bean with a wink.

Bean's dad had built the tree house four summers ago. The envy of every kid on the island, it was located high above the ground in the crotch of a tree. A series of ladders led up to it, and it was entered through a trapdoor in the floor. Inside were bunk beds, a double burner hot plate, two wall lights, a big picture window overlooking the backyard, a smaller window in the south wall, and a little square of carpet, which had been his mother's contribution to the project.

At first Bean spent every summer night in the tree house with one of his friends. Late at night, sometimes after twelve, they would sneak around the neighborhood, hiding from Uncle Phil and anybody else they encountered, which wasn't difficult at that time of night. But it was high adventure.

After a while, though, the novelty wore off, and Bean got tired of hot tea and chicken noodle soup, which were the only things he knew how to cook. So, little by little, the tree house fell into disuse.

Tonight, though, Bean felt that the tree house would play an important role in getting to the bottom of what was going on at the Winthrop House.

"Well, I'm glad to hear it," said Mrs. Carver as she dug out Bean's old sleeping bag from the closet under the stairs. It smelled of mothballs, but Bean didn't mind. "And your father would be, too. You haven't used it in such a long time. I bet it's awfully dusty up there, and the mattresses probably smell of mildew. How about if I—"

"Mom," Bean interrupted. "Spook and me can handle it okay. We're not little kids anymore."

Mrs. Carver relented. "No, I s'pose not. Well," she carried the sleeping bag toward the porch, "at least I can drape this old thing over the railing and let it air out."

Bean rummaged through the drawers and cupboards, assembling everything they would need for the night: Flashlight? Check. Mosquito repellent? Check. Peanut butter and crackers? Check. Sodas? Check. Toothbrush and toothpaste? Nah.

"It's so funny," said Mrs. Carver as she came back in the house, careful not to let the screen door slam, "I was just thinking how you and your friends used to think you were being so smart, sneaking out of the tree house at night and skulking around the neighborhood."

"We did?" said Bean with a lump in his throat.

"Don't you remember? It wasn't that long ago, was it? Of course your dad always followed you to make sure you were all right."

"He did?" said Bean, trying to swallow the lump.

"Sure," said his mom with a laugh. "Didn't you know? Well, I guess that was the fun, wasn't it? Thinking you were out on your own?"

Mrs. Carver continued with a big smile. "You kept your poor dad out awfully late a couple of times." She was thinking that her husband would be home in just three weeks. Then one more tour of duty and he'd be posted at the lighthouse on the island for the rest of his career. She couldn't wait to tell Bean, and she would, as soon as the final papers cleared. "Of course, if it got too late, Uncle Phil would take over."

Uncle Phil knew, too?

"I wish you could have heard him the next morning down at the drugstore. He'd have everybody in stitches talking about how you used to go diving into the pucker brush as soon as you saw his headlights. Then he'd drive on by, go park the truck somewhere, and come back on foot to find out what you were up to and make sure you were okay."

Bean was stunned. He'd thought he and his friends had pulled off the perfect crime. Now it turns out the whole town knew. How humiliating.

By the time he came to his senses, his mother had packed the things he'd collected in a paper bag and managed to slip in his toothbrush and toothpaste without his knowing.

"But you're a lot older now, aren't you?" she said, patting the bag.

"You wouldn't do anything so foolish." Then she winked at him in a meaningful way and squeezed his hand.

What did that mean?

Then, just as enigmatically, she added with a smile, "I doubt poor old Uncle Phil could keep up with you these days." She pressed the bag into his arms. "You take this up, so you don't have to do it later, and straighten up while you're there. At least sweep the cobwebs away. The sleeping bag will be aired out by the time you're ready for bed."

Before he knew which way was up, Bean was stumbling across the backyard toward the tree house. All of a sudden he thought that his idea of sneaking out wasn't such a good one after all. He got the feeling that half the town had been waiting two years for him to do this very thing, just so they'd have something to talk about.

Of course, his mother had been right about something: He was a lot faster now. And, thanks to her, a lot wiser. Uncle Phil would have a hard time keeping up.

By the time he'd climbed, one-handed, to the crotch of the tree and was standing at the foot of the last short stretch of ladder to the trapdoor, Bean had convinced himself that his mother, with all her curious little winks and the comments she'd made, was telling him she knew what he was up to and he'd better be careful.

The trapdoor was a little swollen from the recent fog, so he had to push hard to open it. He poked his head in. The place was just as he'd left it, even if it did wear a layer of dust and smell a little close. Opening the window would take care of that. As he pulled himself through the opening, the old sense of adventure and independence rushed over him, giving him the same goose bumps of excitement he used to get those nights when he and his friends sneaked around town. He laughed. So what if they'd been followed. He'd probably do the same with his kids someday. At least they thought they were having secret adventures, and that made them so.

But tonight it would be different. Tonight he and Spooky would be the ones doing the following.

The tree house was just up the road from the Moses Webster House, and from the little side window Bean and Spooky could see the front of both it and the Winthrop House. By eleven o'clock, they had turned off their lights and set up watch.

The hour that followed seemed the longest in the history of the world. But their wait didn't go unrewarded. At the stroke of twelve, the front door of the Winthrop House opened slowly, sending a pale wash of light onto the lawn. Mierette stepped outside, her every motion wrapped in secrecy.

"This is it," Spooky whispered. "Let's go."

"Wait a second," said Bean sharply, his eyes intent on Mierette's actions. "She's not goin' anywhere."

"What do you mean?"

"She's just standin' there, waitin' for somethin'."

"Monty?"

"Must be."

"Do you see him?" Spooky wedged himself into the window beside Bean.

"Not yet, no . . . wait a second, there he is, comin' out've the bushes across the street."

"I see him," said Spooky.

They watched in silence as Mierette beckoned to Monty, silently reopened the door, and ushered him quickly inside.

"Looks as if we don't do any followin' tonight," said Spooky.

"Things are movin' a lot faster than I thought," Bean said, more to himself than to Spooky.

"Huh?"

"She's snuck him into the house. Maud must be asleep," Bean guessed. "I bet he's gonna search for the treasure. Come on."

"Where we goin'?" Spooky asked as they tumbled down the ladders, leaving the trapdoor open behind them.

"The wood window," said Bean.

"What are you talkin' about?" said Spooky in a loud whisper. By this time they had come to rest in the thick shadows in front of the Winthrop House.

"You gave me the idea," Bean said. By way of explanation he added, "The Moses Webster House has a wood window. This house has fireplaces, too. They must use wood—"

"So it must have a wood window," Spooky concluded excitedly.

"Now all we have to do is find it."

"No problem," said Spooky. "It'll be in back, near the street. That's where they dump the wood."

The window was easily found. It occupied a position smack in the middle of the cellar wall under the kitchen annex at the back of the house. To make things better, it was easy to see that the window was open. This was often the case during the summer in order to increase air circulation and cut down on the growth of mold and mildew. The situation wasn't perfect, though; a particularly bright street lamp stood atop a telephone pole between the boys and the window, and any attempt they made to cross that sea of light would immediately attract the attention of a casual observer on either side of the street.

The fact that few casual observers would be around at this time of the night was, of course, in the boys' favor. But it wouldn't take a crowd; one would be enough. And Bean had no difficulty imagining how unimpressed Ab's parents would be if he was caught trying to sneak into the Winthrop House. Should that happen, his chances of getting back into their good graces were about the same as a pollack being elected president of the fishermen's co-op.

It was not, therefore, with a light heart that Bean contemplated the next move.

Spooky, too, saw the problem. "What're we gonna do?" he asked. "It's like daylight out there. We might as well knock on the front door and walk in."

Bean grabbed hold of Spooky's words. "You're right!"

"I am?"

"That's just what we should do. Create a diversion." Bean had become a great believer in diversionary tactics, owing to recent success. "It's pretty dark out front of both places. You go to the front door of Maud's place, and I'll go to the front door here," he tossed a nod over his shoulder at the Moses Webster House. "When I give a whistle, you ring the bell a couple of times and run like crazy 'round the other side of the house, then come back and meet me here. Anybody who's up at this time of night will want to know who's at the door so late. By the time they figure out nobody's there—"

"We'll be through the wood window," said Spooky. "It's big enough." He was impressed with Bean. He'd never suspected him of being a tactical genius. "Let's go for it."

Spooky retraced his steps around the dark side of the Winthrop House while Bean rounded the other side of the Moses Webster House, where he made his way to the front door. From there he could see Spooky in place next door. Bean gave one sharp, low whistle and rang the doorbell. He heard it echo through the sleeping house, but the sound hadn't died before he abandoned his post and was flying around the corner, almost colliding with a low branch of the giant lilac bush that grew beside the path.

Seconds later he had hidden himself at the rendezvous point, panting puffs of steam into the cool night air. Where was Spooky?

Lights came on in the Moses Webster House and marked the trail of whoever had gotten up to answer the door: upstairs bedroom, upstairs hall, stairway, kitchen. Two more rooms to go.

Where was Spooky? The lights came on in the dining room and front hall.

"Ready?" said a voice at Bean's elbow. It was Spooky.

"Where have you been?" asked Bean as he settled slowly back into his skin.

"I hadda pee," Spooky replied.

"Great," said Bean. "Now we've got about two seconds to get over there and in the window. Come on."

He grabbed Spooky by the sleeve and ran across the hollow. Seconds later they were through the window, watching breathlessly behind them to see if they'd been discovered. One by one the lights in the Moses Webster House went off as whoever had gotten up to answer the door headed back to bed.

"I don't think anybody saw us," said Bean.

They listened intently for another thirty seconds and were rewarded with silence. "Okay," said Spooky. "The coast is clear."

Bean turned on the flashlight, directing it at the floor to avoid detection from outside. They were about to begin their exploration when, all at once, a sound overhead froze them in their tracks.

"Somebody's comin'," said Spooky.

Bean flicked off the flashlight.

Somewhere in the darkness above, a door squeaked open and stealthy footsteps began descending the stairs. Mierette and Monty spoke in hushed whispers, and the candles they carried threw long, wavering shadows on the irregular walls and pilings.

"This is spooky," said Spooky in his lowest possible whisper.

Bean nudged Spooky to a place under the stairway. Through large cracks in the treads, they could watch clearly without being seen.

"There was nobody there," said Mierette.

"Kids playin' pranks," Monty theorized.

"What do we do now?" said Mierette.

Monty was inspecting the walls closely, every now and then rapping them sharply with a crowbar. "Just like I figured," he said, more to himself than Mierette. He was running his hand over the granite of the north wall of the cellar. "A false wall," he proclaimed.

"False wall? Thees means what?" said Mierette.

Monty, startled from his thoughts, flashed her a surprised glance, as if he'd forgotten she was there. "What?" he said. "Oh . . ." He seemed to be deliberating whether or not to take Mierette into his confidence. "This wall is fake," he said finally, tugging at a loose piece of stone. It came away in his hand, revealing a small triangle of plasterboard. "See? This isn't the outside wall, but somebody sure wanted to make it look that way."

"I don't undarestan'," said Mierette. "What dees means?"

"Dees means," Monty mimicked, "that there's space between the walls."

"A room?"

"Must be. Or the tunnel."

"Thees ees whare she paints dee pictures, then," said Mierette. "Dee studio."

Monty wasn't prepared to speculate any further. He tapped the wall again. "If there's a room here, there's got to be a way in. Where could it be?"

Mierette shrugged. "I don' kno. Madam says to me, 'turn around and face dee wall, Mierette.' I do. And when I turn again, she ees gone." She snapped her fingers. "Like dees. Poof. I teenk maybe she is ghost, eh?"

Monty ran the candle close to the wall. "She may be a spook," he said, "but she's no more a ghost than you and me. Take my word for it, there's a door somewhere."

At one point in his investigation, Monty came within two feet of the boys' hiding place beneath the stairs. They held their breath. As little respect as Bean had for Monty as a person, he knew he was strong, and he'd seen him lose his temper. Not a pretty sight. Bean sure didn't want to be on the receiving end of his cousin's anger. The boys pressed back against the wall as far as possible.

"Not here," Monty pronounced finally.

"Den whare?" Mierette questioned eagerly. "Whare cood eet be?"

"Maybe there's something behind the stairs," said Monty as he began to walk straight to where the boys were hidden.

Bean's Adam's apple rose promptly to his throat and stuck there. He felt Spooky lock onto his elbow and squeeze. He shook his arm, but Spooky wouldn't come loose.

16

One More Mystery

"Who's there?" said a voice from the top of the stairs. It was Maud.

Now it was Monty's turn to panic. Quickly he blew out his candle, but Mierette kept hers burning.

Bean couldn't see any way out. In just a few seconds, they'd all be caught. But one person remained cool and calm: Mierette. She went to the bottom of the stairs, looked up, and curtsied politely. *"C'est moi, mam'selle,"* she said. Bean noticed how composed she was. Her words were clear and casual. She wasn't blushing, and her eyes weren't watering the way his and Spooky's and Monty's were. *"Je n'tombe pas. Je pense qui j'ecout quelque chose ici."* She held up the crowbar that Monty, hidden in the shadows, had hastily thrust in her hand.

"What kind of noise?" Maud demanded.

"J'ne sais pas," Mierette replied, still showing no lack of confidence. "A bump, I teenk. Bot dere ees notting here. *Rien.*"

"Where did the sound come from?" asked Maud sharply, a little edge to her voice.

Mierette pointed innocently at the false wall. "Dees wall, I teenk. De noise, she stops as I come down."

"You go back to bed now," Maud commanded. Instantly she was gone.

For the next few seconds, Bean and Spooky, Monty and Mierette waited breathlessly. Then Monty spoke in a harsh whisper. "What did you tell her that for?"

Mierette calmly held a finger to her lips and a hand to her ear. *"Ecoutez,"* she said. "Listen."

For a moment there was nothing to hear. Then the sound of footsteps, barely audible, came through the false wall.

Mierette smiled. Although Monty couldn't see the smile, because she was turned away from him, Bean could. It was a smile that revealed something unexpected about the girl. All of a sudden she didn't seem so simple and innocent. Now what do you suppose she's up to? Bean thought to himself.

There was no time, however, for further speculation. Monty crowded next to the wall and pressed his ear against it.

"I can hear her in there," he whispered. "There must be another way down. A hidden stairway somewhere."

"Eet mos' be op here," said Mierette, starting up the stairs. Monty followed her closely.

Leaving enough time for everyone to get beyond earshot, Bean and Spooky crawled out from under the stairs and stood waiting in the darkness. For several seconds, they heard only the faint sounds of shuffling, both overhead and beyond the wall, but not enough in either case to tell what was going on.

"Up," said Bean abruptly, nudging Spooky in the ribs. They ascended the stairs, placing their feet as close as possible to the sides of the steps in order to keep them from squeaking.

At the top of the stairs, they found the door closed, but there was a wide gap under the door through which they could clearly see what was going on in the hall.

At the moment, Monty and Mierette were standing nose to nose and talking in hasty whispers. The boys couldn't make out any words, but the result of the conference was that Monty hid himself in a closet and Mierette hustled up the stairs, which the boys could hear creaking overhead.

Mierette didn't go to her room, though. Bean could tell that she had stopped near the top of the stairs, as if she were waiting for something.

"What are they waiting for?" whispered Spooky.

No sooner had he finished the question than Bean heard the sound of footsteps on a stairway. For half a second, he thought that Mierette must be coming back downstairs. Then he realized that the sound was coming from the other side of the wall to his left—the false wall. "It's Maud," Bean said in Spooky's ear. He directed his attention to the hall.

"She's comin' back," said Spooky.

"Shh."

"What if she comes back here?"

"Shh!"

The footsteps were nearing the top of the stairs.

"We gotta get outta here," said Spooky. He was about to bolt down the stairs, but Bean, still staring through the crack under the door, grabbed him by the sleeve and pulled him down. "Shh," he repeated. "Watch."

Spooky bent close to the crack and peeled his eyes.

The footsteps stopped momentarily. Then a panel on the wall to their left swung slowly and silently open. Maud, looking carefully about her, stepped into the hall, carefully closed the panel behind her, and walked to the bottom of the main stairs.

"Just as Ab said," Bean whispered.

"Mierette," Maud called.

From upstairs the maid replied. Her voice sounded tired, as if she were yawning. *"Oui, mam'selle?"*

Maud hesitated a moment. "Nothing," she said finally. "Go to bed. If you hear anything else, let me know. Don't go down to the cellar by yourself. *Tu comprends?*"

"Oui, mam'selle," Mierette replied meekly. *"Bon soir."*

"Good-night," said Maud coolly.

Maud returned to the hallway outside the cellar door. For a moment it looked as if Spooky's prophesy were about to come true. Instead of returning to the cellar, though, she stood indecisively for a second and listened.

It seemed a long time until she finally moved again—a long time during which Spooky found it hard to breathe, and Bean was sure his heart was beating loud enough to be heard a block away. At last she went to the wall and flipped a switch, shutting off the ceiling light and leaving only a dim bulb in the wall sconce to light her way upstairs.

Bean knew what was going to happen next. No doubt Monty had been watching from his hiding place and had discovered Maud's secret passage. He would wait a few minutes, until he was sure the coast was clear, then make his way to the tunnel and search for the treasure.

But what would he find? Just what Ab had found. Paintings, frames, and blank canvasses.

"What're we waiting for?" said Spooky.

Bean held his finger to his lips. "Shh. Watch."

Spooky did, and soon his watching was rewarded. A door on the opposite side of the hall swung slowly open, with just the faintest squeak, and Monty stepped into the hallway. He hesitated only a moment, then made his way to the secret panel and ran his hands along the molding. Finding the piece that doubled as a switch, he pressed it. The hidden door popped open without a sound and, in a second, he was gone.

What happened next, Bean hadn't expected. Mierette was in the hallway again. He hadn't even heard her on the stairs. She quickly crossed to the secret panel, pressed the molding, stepped into the darkness, and pulled the panel closed behind her.

"What's she up to?" Bean wondered aloud.

"What if we follow 'em?" Spooky suggested.

Bean didn't like that idea. "Too risky," he said. "Only one way out, and there's no way I want to be caught down there with Monty."

"I know," said Spooky. Without another word, he had flicked on the flashlight and was on his way back down to the cellar. Bean wanted to call after him and ask him what he was doing, but everyone in the house would have heard. Instead, as quietly as possible, he followed.

Spooky was rummaging around in the dirt. "What are you looking for?" Bean demanded in a loud whisper.

Spooky didn't answer, but after a few seconds he produced a long, rusty spike, which he held up triumphantly. "Ta-da!" he said beneath his breath as he shone his light on his treasure.

"So?"

Spooky gestured to the wall, found the place from which Monty had removed the chip of stone, and began digging at the plasterboard with the spike. Bean was about to object, but before he could get the words out, the deed was done. Spooky withdrew the spike and applied his eye to the hole.

"Perfect," he said softly.

Bean swallowed his objection. "What do you see?" he said, pressing his head as close to Spooky's as physics would allow.

"They're feelin' around the walls, tryin' to find somethin'."

"The switch," said Bean. "Ab told me there's another hidden switch that opens the tunnel door."

"They got it," Spooky exclaimed aloud. Fortunately for them, Mierette said, "I found eet" at the exact same time.

Bean clamped his hand over Spooky's mouth. "Don't do that," he commanded in a sharp whisper. "Let me see." He pushed Spooky gently aside and pressed his eye to the hole. Mierette was just removing her hand from the slot in the old timber. The second secret door was mostly open, and Monty was already through it. A moment later a light came on in the tunnel.

"What's happenin'?" said Spooky.

Bean didn't reply. Instead he watched intently as first Monty, then Mierette disappeared through the door. "I wish I could see what they're doin'." A few seconds later, it was obvious. The sinister duo emerged from the tunnel carrying armloads of canvasses. "Mostly blanks," Bean said in a low voice.

"What?" said Spooky. "What're they doin'?"

Bean turned away from the wall and scratched his head. "It looks as if they're stealin' stuff—paintings and blank canvasses."

Spooky stuck his eye against the hole. "Blank canvasses?" He watched carefully. "Why?" He, too, turned away in bewilderment. He looked at Bean, who shrugged.

"Ab said that's the first thing Maud went after when she thought there was a fire."

"Canvas ain't that hard to come by, is it?" Spooky asked.

Something about the comment nudged Bean's thoughts a little further down the track. "No," he said. "You can get 'em down to the paper store and the hardware store both." He thought a little longer. "But she saved 'em before she saved some've her own paintings. That means . . ." Something was on the tip of his tongue. "That means they must be worth somethin'."

"But you just said blank canvasses are easy to come by. That means they ain't worth much. Sure not worth riskin' your life for," Spooky rightly theorized.

Bean was forced to an inevitable conclusion. "So they're not what they look like."

"Huh?"

"They're not blank canvasses," said Bean.

Spooky returned to the hole and, squinting, peered at the hidden tunnel. "They sure look blank to me."

"They're s'posed to," said Bean, following the train of thought with increasing excitement. "But they're not. So either they're not really canvasses or they're not really blank."

Once again he pushed Spooky aside and stared through the hole. "Some of 'em are turned toward us and some are turned away. I can see both sides. They're canvasses, all right."

"Then they're not really blank?" asked Spooky.

"That's right," said Bean. "Either they're paintings that've been painted over, or—"

"They're paintings that've been covered over with new canvas," Spooky deduced.

"That's it!" said Bean, managing to stifle his enthusiasm only at the last second. "'Every one a masterpiece.'"

"What're you talkin' about?"

"Maud's motto down at her gallery. 'Every painting a masterpiece.' What if she stole a bunch of paintings from a museum or somethin', like this place down in Boston that me and Ab read about in an old newspaper. And what if she put new canvas over 'em, so they couldn't be found?"

Spooky was one or two steps ahead. "Then she painted her paintings on the new canvas?"

"Right."

"Then she put the paintings in her gallery?"

"Right."

"Then she sold 'em for hardly nothin' to people who didn't know they were really buyin' a masterpiece?"

Bean saw the difficulty in this. "Doesn't make any sense, does it?"

"Not to me, it don't," said Spooky.

Bean had really thought he was onto something, but he couldn't see his way around this obstacle in his logic. "Not to me either," he said. He turned once again and peered through the hole. "They're closin' the secret door. They must've got it all."

"What're we gonna do now?"

Bean was thinking frantically as he watched Mierette and Monty carry some of the canvasses up the stairs. He could read Mierette's lips as she said, "Pleeze be carefool."

"They're takin' 'em upstairs just a few at a time. It's gonna take 'em a minute or two," he said.

Spooky didn't consider this an answer. "What're we gonna do?"

Bean said the only thing that came to mind: "Follow 'em. Come on." He bounded up the stairs as quietly as possible, and Spooky followed close on his heels.

Bean surveyed the hallway carefully through the crack under the door at the top of the stairs. "Coast is clear," he said and, turning the knob with shaky fingers, pushed the door open.

In seconds they had closed the cellar door behind them and made their way across the hall to the closet where Monty had hidden earlier.

They left the door open a crack to watch. At that instant, Monty and Mierette appeared through the hidden panel with the first of the canvasses and carried them toward the kitchen.

"They're goin' out the back," said Bean. "If I'd known, we coulda gone out to the barn and waited for 'em."

Spooky didn't reply.

"Spook?" said Bean.

Still no answer. Bean held out his hand and rummaged through the darkness. "Spooky?" There were overcoats, raincoats, boots, hats, and shoes, but from one end of the closet to the other, no sign of Spooky.

As Bean, in the height of alarm, was ransacking the farthest recesses of the closet, he suddenly felt a tap on his shoulder. He would have screamed, but his Adam's apple was wedged in his throat, so he couldn't.

"I found another way out," said Spooky, unaware that he'd nearly given his friend heart failure. "Over here." He tugged Bean to the end of the closet, where he opened a sliding panel in the wall to their left. "This used to be a butler's pantry," he said. "There's two pass-throughs—this one and one over where you were that goes to the dinin' room."

Bean was familiar with pass-throughs: tiny panels in the walls that slid up and down so the cook could pass food through to the pantry and the butler could pass it through to the dining room sideboard without interrupting the people who were having dinner.

"This one goes to the kitchen?" Bean said as Spooky raised the panel slightly.

"Yeah," said Spooky. "I been through once, but she almost caught me when she brung some pictures in."

"Mierette?"

"Yeah."

"Then we gotta time this just right," whispered Bean. He stepped to the door and peered through the crack. "They carry most of the loads together, so as soon as they come out of the kitchen after the next load, we'll dive through and get out to the barn. Okay?"

"Okay," Spooky agreed.

"You stay there. As soon as I tell you, open 'er up."

"Got it," said Spooky. Their conversation had been carried on in the softest whispers, which were further muffled by the heavy winter coats that hung in their faces.

Bean timed their escape perfectly. The instant that Monty followed Mierette out of the kitchen after the next load, Bean said, "Go." A split second later, Spooky was halfway through the pass-through. Unfortunately, one of the recently placed paintings in the kitchen slid on the linoleum, making a loud clap as it hit the floor. Mierette and Monty froze in their tracks. Spooky froze halfway into the pass-through.

Bean watched as Mierette and Monty waited breathlessly to see if Maud had heard. Finally, Mierette seemed satisfied that they hadn't been discovered, and she prodded Monty toward the hidden panel. Monty was shaken, and all the color had drained from his face, but he complied.

"Go," Bean whispered sharply. Spooky slithered through the opening, and Bean followed. Once in the kitchen, they shut the pass-through behind them and ran to the little passageway that connected the house to the barn. Bean reached for the door handle and pulled, but nothing happened. "It's locked," he hissed.

"Someone's comin'," said Spooky.

Beads of sweat immediately broke out on Bean's forehead. The door had some play in it. There must be a hook-and-eye latch somewhere. Frantically he traced the molding with his fingers.

"Found it," he whispered as the hook rattled in the eye.

"Too late," said Spooky.

17

SUDDENLY AT SEA

THE KITCHEN DOOR SWUNG OPEN and Mierette and Monty entered with the last load of canvasses. Bean knew that their eyes would take a few seconds to adjust to the dark, so, seizing the momentary advantage, he grabbed Spooky and pulled him in among some raincoats that hung in a little nook beside the back door. "Stand still," he whispered in Spooky's ear.

Mierette's and Monty's exchange of excited whispers drowned out the faint rustling of the boys pressing themselves into the shadows. "I have deez," said Mierette. "Go and open dee dor. Eet has a leetle hook on dee lef' side."

Monty, with one armful of paintings, tiptoed to the door and, standing so close that Bean could hear him breathing, fumbled in the darkness for the latch. "I can't find the hook," he whispered sharply. "Flick on the light for half a second."

Spooky instinctively clamped Beans elbow and squeezed.

"Don' be foolish," said Mierette, much to Bean's relief. "Eet ees dere, near de top."

Finally Monty found the hook, popped it out of the eye, and pushed the door open. Instantly the little passageway was filled with a wave of musty smells from the unused barn.

Bean and Spooky flattened themselves against the wall as Mierette, her arms full of paintings, crowded beside Monty. "Go on," she commanded, nudging him with her shoulder. "Hurry."

A loop of twine hung by a nail on the wall. In one smooth motion, Mierette slipped the knot over the latch so the door couldn't swing shut as she and Monty made their way back and forth between the barn and the kitchen with the paintings. In one of these intervals, Monty stepped on the toe of Bean's sneaker, but Bean was much too frightened to cry out in pain.

"What's that?" said Monty suspiciously.

"Wot ees wot?"

"I stepped on somethin' down here." Monty began to grope around in the darkness, his fingers finally lighting on Bean's sneaker. He picked it up, fortunately not before Bean had been able to slip his foot out of it.

"Just an old sneaker," he said. He sniffed it. "Phew."

"Neever mind dat," said Mierette impatiently. "Get deez paintings down to dee bateau."

They transferred the remainder of the paintings to the barn without further incident. Mierette and Monty were framed in the doorway. "Whare eez de trock?"

"Parked on the other side of that lilac bush, like you said," said Monty.

"You can handle dees yourself now?"

Monty was offended. "'Course I can. Five minutes I'll have 'em all loaded an' be on my way down to the shore."

"Dee bateau, eet ees ready?"

"Don't you worry about that," Monty snapped impatiently.

"Shh," Mierette cautioned, holding her hand to his mouth.

"Don't you worry about that," Monty repeated softly through her fingers. "I'll get 'em out to the island all right. What I want to know is, how long we gonna keep 'em out there?"

"They weel stay dere ontil dee heat ees over."

"Off. Heat is off," Monty corrected. "What about the money? I ain't gonna wait forever, you know."

Mierette softened suddenly. "Som teengs air wort dee wait, *n'est-ce pas?*" She gave him a quick kiss and he settled down.

"Well," said Monty, "I guess there ain't no rush."

"Dat eez right," said Mierette. "When she have stop looking, dat ees when we start to sell dem. But you mos' be patient, no? Eet weel take time. Now, you go. I mos' be ready eef she calls."

"Better you than me," said Monty. He tried to kiss her, but she stopped him.

"Der ees no time now," she said. "Go on."

She pushed him gently away, quickly pulled the door closed, and latched it.

For a minute or so she stood with her ear to the door, listening to make sure that Monty was carrying out her orders. Meanwhile, Bean and Spooky held their breath.

Apparently satisfied, Mierette stole silently across the kitchen and opened the hall door. For an instant she was silhouetted against the rectangle of light. She wiped her mouth with the back of her hand, then turned and was gone. The door swung shut with just the faintest click, and Bean and Spooky were enveloped in silence.

"What now?" asked Spooky at last.

Just what Bean had been wondering. "I dunno."

"What island is he goin' to?"

"I dunno," Bean replied.

"Do you know anything?" Spooky said a little impatiently.

It came to Bean in a flash. "He keeps his boat down at Sands Cove. We can get there before him, while he's loadin' the truck."

Spooky objected. "That's two miles."

"No problem," Bean said confidently. "First thing we gotta do is get outta here."

"We can't go out this way," said Spooky. "Monty's in the barn."

"And we can't go out that way," said Bean, nodding toward the kitchen door. "Mierette's prob'ly still out there."

"I'd rather face her than ol' Maud," said Spook with a shiver.

"Out the window," Bean decided abruptly. Before Spooky could say "huh?" Bean had crossed the kitchen to the south side of the house and wedged his fingers under the window.

Expecting the window to be stuck, like most windows in old houses, Bean gave a sharp pull. He was stunned when, aided by clanging counterweights, it flew up with a bang. Half a second later, with his heart pounding in his ears, he dove through the window. Dragging himself off the grass, he poked his head up over the sill. "Come on," he whispered harshly.

"What are you waitin' for?" said Spooky from the street.

Bean did a double take and rubbed his eyes. "How'd you do that?"

"Come on."

This was no time for questions. Bean took to his heels. Seeing that Spooky had jumped into some roadside bushes, he joined him.

"Now," said Spooky, huffing and puffing, "how're we gonna get to the boat before Monty does?"

"No problem," said Bean, drawing his sleeve across his sweaty forehead. "We've got the Blue Moose."

"We've got a blue what?"

Bean had extricated himself from the bushes and, keeping to the deepest shadows, was headed toward home, with Spooky following close behind. "The Blue Moose," Bean repeated over his shoulder.

"What's that?" said Spooky.

Five minutes later Spooky had his answer. "Cool," he said as he climbed on the moped and twisted the throttle a couple of times. "Fire 'er up."

"Shh," said Bean. They were only a few feet from his mother's bedroom window, and he knew she was a light sleeper. He tugged Spooky off the bike. "We'll wheel it to the top of the hill near the net factory and jump-start it there, so we don't wake up my mom."

Just then, in the near distance, they heard the sound of an engine starting. "That's Monty," said Bean quietly. "He's already loaded." Bean knew they had only seconds to spare. "Come on."

They each took hold of the bike and ran it to the hill. Bean hopped on and turned the key. "Give it to 'er," said Spooky, climbing on behind.

Halfway down the hill, Bean popped the clutch on the handlebar. The little one-cylinder engine burped loudly once or twice amid puffs of acrid blue smoke. "All right!" cried Spooky gleefully.

But the Blue Moose didn't start. Not only were they running out of hill, from the corner of his eye Bean caught the flash of headlights in Frog Hollow. In a few seconds Monty would be right behind them.

Bean popped the clutch again. There were more burps this time, and more smoke, but the moped still didn't start. "She's flooded," Bean said with alarm.

"I musta done that when I twisted the throttle," Spooky volunteered apologetically.

The Blue Moose rolled to a standstill against a high ledge of sidewalk in front of the Islander Cafe. "What now?" said Spooky.

"Hop off," Bean ordered as he jumped off himself. With his foot he flipped out the foot pad on the starter pedal and began pumping it for all he was worth. Once or twice the reluctant engine seemed about to start, but it didn't.

Headlights flashed on the road beside them. "Too late," said Bean. "Grab hold."

Quickly the boys grabbed the bike from the front and back, lifted it onto the sidewalk, and dragged it into the shadow of the steps leading to the cafe. And not a second too soon. The rear wheel had just disappeared into the shadows when Monty's truck burst around the corner, framing all of Main Street in its headlights. In no time, the boys were watching tail lights as the truck drove out of town.

Spooky stepped from the shadows. "No way we'll catch him now," he said.

Bean pulled the bike to the edge of the sidewalk. "Help me get this down," he said. They placed the moped on the pavement. "He's still got to unload the truck."

Once again Bean pumped the starter pedal furiously.

"She don't sound as if she wants to start," Spooky observed, not too helpfully.

Bean cast him a withering glance and kept on pumping.

Finally, as if the Blue Moose knew that Bean was about to give up, she sputtered to life. "Pile on," Bean cried as he straddled the bike and gave the throttle a couple of sharp twists. The bike backfired once or twice in response, and they were on their way.

The dirt road that twisted through the thick growth of pine, juniper, and blackberry bushes to Monty's fish house was pitted with deep potholes. Bean artfully negotiated these to within a hundred yards of the shore, where he cut the engine. "Let's go the rest of the way on foot."

They hid the Blue Moose among the thick branches of an old pine tree.

Rounding the next bend, they saw Monty's truck. In its headlights was Bean's cousin bustling back and forth, ferrying paintings to his lobster boat, which was tied at the dock with its powerful engine rumbling softly.

"Good," said Bean. "He's just gettin' started."

"How do you know?"

"Simple," said Bean. "He keeps his boat out on the moorin'. That means he had to row out and get it. That took ten minutes, I bet."

"What're we gonna do now?"

Without his even being conscious of it, an idea had taken shape in Bean's mind. "Follow me," he said. "You'll see."

Spooky fell in behind Bean as he threaded his way down a narrow path to the shore. From there, they scrambled from rock to rock, careful to keep the old granite pier and its mussel-encrusted pilings between themselves and Monty.

Fortunately it was low tide, so the boys could stick to the shore and, using a leaky old punt as a bridge, hop across to the float without having to go up on the pier and down the ramp. "Quick," said Bean as he boarded Monty's boat. "He's comin'."

The door in the main bulkhead was already open, so the boys dodged into the trunk cabin where the powerful engine throbbed smoothly. The air was thick with the smell of oil and fresh paint.

Their eyes quickly became accustomed to the faint glow of a small flashlight Monty left on the bunk. "Uh-oh," said Bean.

"I hate when you say that," said Spooky. "What's wrong now?"

"Look." Bean pointed at the port bow, where six or seven of the paintings leaned under the decking. "This is where he's stackin' 'em."

Just then they heard the sound of a heavy footstep on the gunwale. Stooping to avoid smashing their heads, the boys scudded around to the starboard side of the engine and huddled in the shadows.

Fear rose in their throats as Monty's footsteps approached. He was visible in the weak light as he ducked through the opening with an armload of canvasses, which he deposited carefully beside the others.

He was just headed back out when Spooky's foot, which had been wedged against the engine block, slipped against the console wall with a loud thud.

Monty stopped in his tracks and cocked his head. Luckily the rhythmic pulse of the engine had absorbed most of the sound, so it could have been anything from a distant peal of thunder to a piece of driftwood bumping against the hull. Clearly Monty was unsure. Once more the boys found themselves holding their breath as they watched him listening. He bent his ear toward the engine. At last, apparently satisfied that nothing was seriously wrong, he muttered something under his breath and went back outside.

"Phew," the boys exhaled in unison.

"That was close," Bean said, sighing.

"Too close," Spooky emphasized. "Ain't there someplace else to hide?"

Bean searched the compartment with squinted eyes. So did Spooky.

"Hey," said Spooky, "what's that?"

Bean saw a little panel in the forward bulkhead. "The chain locker," he said. "Perfect."

Two short pieces of wood, screwed snugly to the bulkhead on each side of the chain locker panel, held the panel in place. In half a second the boys had turned the pieces of wood and, using the little brass handle on the panel, lifted it aside to reveal the inside of the locker. It was crowded with ropes, chains, bailers, and life jackets.

Spooky surveyed the prospects doubtfully. "There ain't much room to hide in," he said.

For an instant Bean thought it might be best to abandon the idea and return to the shadows beside the engine. But it was too late. Footsteps announced Monty's imminent return.

"Quick," Bean commanded in a sharp whisper. "Get in."

He pushed Spooky through the little opening, and kept pushing until he had disappeared. "Hitch over," he said.

"There ain't nowhere to hitch," Spooky replied.

Monty was just outside the door. In another two seconds, he'd be in the engine room. Two seconds after that, his eyes would have grown accustomed to the darkness. Bean stuck his head in the chain locker, grabbed the hook that held the boat end of the anchor chain, and dragged himself into the cramped compartment, putting arms and legs wherever they'd fit. "Grab the cover," he ordered.

Spooky forced a hand through the tangle of limbs and fumbled around on the floor outside until his fingers touched the brass handle. He pulled the panel into place just as Monty's feet appeared in the passageway.

Somewhere in the darkness, Bean sighed again. "I think I'm about to have a heart attack," he said softly, not afraid of being heard over the steady thrumming of the engine.

"I hope he don't see that the handle ain't closed," Spooky replied.

Bean swallowed a lump in his throat. "Thanks," he said. "I almost forgot."

"And the handle's on the wrong side," Spooky continued. He was using the handle to hold the panel in place.

"You ain't helpin' much," Bean said.

A minute later, though, the engine revved up.

"We're off," said Spooky.

They relaxed as much as possible. As it was, Bean's elbow was in Spooky's ear. As their legs and arms fell asleep in their contorted positions, the boys couldn't tell which belonged to whom.

Two minutes later the waves of the open sea were beating regularly against the bow. "I can't stay like this," Bean said finally. He was having a hard time taking a deep breath and was starting to feel claustrophobic. "I gotta get out." He forced his fingers onto the handle beside Spooky's and pushed the panel away from the opening.

"Where you gonna go?" said Spooky. Not that he was sad to have a little more room to himself. He stretched his arms and legs as far as space would allow and thrilled to the tingle as the blood rushed back into them.

"Back beside the engine," said Bean. "I'll put the panel back the way it's s'posed to be and let you out when we get to the island."

Spooky didn't think much of the idea, but he saw that it made sense. "Okay," he said. "But don't forget me, or I'll kick it out."

"Don't worry," said Bean as he slipped the panel into place and held it fast by turning the pieces of wood.

He tucked himself back in the shadows on the starboard side of the engine, where it was warm. In a few minutes he began to feel drowsy as the boat rose and fell easily on the gentle swells, like a huge motorized cradle. He must have dozed, because he was suddenly awakened by the sound of the throttle backing off. For a second he forgot where he was. When he remembered, his heart once more rose to his throat.

Must be at the island, he said to himself. Which one, though? There were literally dozens of uninhabited islands scattered across the bay, and he didn't know if they'd been gone minutes or hours. They could be anywhere. Through the door in the main bulkhead he could see that it was still pitch dark outside, so he figured they hadn't been gone too long.

His thoughts were interrupted when he tipped to one side as the boat, with its engine cut to an easy idle, nudged hard against a fixed object. A float, Bean thought as he righted himself. That meant an inhabited island, which cut the possibilities by about 80 percent. He heard Monty jump off the boat and tie the bow line to a ring in the float. He didn't tie the stern line, which meant they were probably facing upwind; otherwise the stern would have drifted away from the float and swung the boat around.

The wind was supposed to be out of the southeast, Bean remembered from the last weather he'd heard on the radio. That meant they were on the leeward side of an island, facing southeast. Not that that meant a lot, but every little piece of information might come in handy later on.

Further speculation was cut short by the sound of Monty jumping back aboard. Bean scrunched himself tightly into the shadows and listened as Monty made a beeline for the trunk cabin and the paintings.

Once again, Monty shifted the paintings—this time from boat to land—while Bean watched and waited from the cover of his hiding place, his heart keeping time with the steady throb of the engine.

In four trips, Monty had unloaded all but three or four of the paintings. He'd be back one more time, Bean figured. Good. Bean's legs were cramped, and he wanted to stretch. He was thankful that he hadn't stayed in the chain locker with Spooky.

Apparently Monty wasn't taking the paintings farther than the float, because there was little time between trips. Bean knew that this meant he'd be making more trips back and forth from the float to wherever he was going to hide them. That would give Bean time to think and plan, and let Spooky out of the chain locker.

Bean was so deep in thought that he was startled when Monty came for the last load of canvasses. In his hurry to get out of the way, Bean bumped his head against a hot pipe and just barely managed to stifle a cry.

Suddenly there was a loud sneeze. It came from the chain locker. Monty froze in place. "What's that?" he said, cocking his head. "Who's there?" He reached over to the engine and pulled the choke. The engine quickly sputtered and died, leaving a huge, deep silence. For a second it seemed as though Monty were about to convince himself he'd been hearing things. Unfortunately, Spooky sneezed again. Louder this time.

18

Caught in the Act

It took about two seconds for Monty to open the panel in the bulkhead and pull Spooky, kicking and squirming, from his hiding place.

"Spooky Martin, what the heck are you doin'?" said Monty, his brain apparently racing to catch up with this unexpected turn of events. "How long you been in there?" He shook Spooky good and hard.

"Hey," said Spooky, emboldened by fear. "You're rattlin' my eyeballs. Let me go." He tore himself from Monty's grasp. "I ain't done nothin'."

"What're you doin' on my boat?" Monty demanded.

Bean was wrestling with two options. He could either come to Spooky's rescue and give everything away, or wait to see if a better opportunity might develop. He decided to wait. And while he waited, he prayed that Spooky wouldn't give him away.

"I was hidin'," Spooky replied, as if he were the injured party.

"Hidin' from what?"

Never had Bean been so thankful that Monty was not a quick thinker.

"Bean," said Spooky.

Bean almost leaped from the shadows.

"What d'you mean? Beanbag?"

"Yeah. We was sleepin' out in his tree house and went out for a sneak-around. We met up with some other kids down around Sands Cove and decided to play hide-and-seek," Spooky said calmly. The story was apparently making itself up as he went along. "Bean was It, and the rest of us went and hid." He paused for a moment. "I hid in here while you was loadin'."

"Loadin' what?" said Monty suspiciously.

Spooky shrugged. "How do I know? I wasn't watchin' you. I was lookin' out for Bean."

There was only one problem with this explanation, thought Bean. If Spooky hid himself in the chain locker, how had the pieces of wood been turned shut? Of course, there was a good chance that the thought would never occur to Monty.

"Hey," said Monty. "If you hid yourself in there, how did the handles get closed?"

Bean shook his head, but Spooky hesitated for only a second. "One of the other kids shut me in," he said. "He was gonna let me out if Bean didn't find me."

"So, what happened?" Monty demanded.

"I fell asleep," said Spooky matter-of-factly. "Next thing I know, you're draggin' me outta there and shakin' me all over the place. Now, lemme go."

"Let you go?" Monty repeated. "Where d'you think you are?"

"At your float," Spooky said.

Bean wondered what Spooky was up to.

"You mean, you been asleep the whole time?" said Monty, taking Spooky by the shoulders again. "You don't remember anything?"

"What's to remember?" said Spooky. "What time is it? They're gonna be lookin' for me."

Monty laughed. "Well, they ain't gonna find you. Look out there." He pushed Spooky to one of the trunk cabin's portlights.

"Hey," cried Spooky in perfect surprise. "This ain't Sands Cove." He turned and faced Monty. "Where are we?"

"Ha!" said Monty. "I guess what you don't know won't hurt ya. You get out and give me some help."

He pushed Spooky out of the cabin, off the boat, and onto the float. Now that the engine was off, Bean could make out what they were saying. "Grab an armload've these things and follow me," ordered Monty.

Bean waited a second, then raised his head and stared out the starboard portlight. In the first faint hint of dawn, he could make out a ramp leading to a small island. Monty and Spooky were carrying the canvasses up a steep, narrow path into the woods.

"What now?" he said to himself. "Think, think." He tapped his head. A lot of possibilities ran through his brain at high speed. What if he followed them? But why should he? He knew they were going to some camp up in the woods where Monty and Mierette had conspired to hide the canvasses. And there couldn't be more than one or two camps on an island this size. So, what if he waited until Monty left, then went in and stole the canvasses? But what would he do with them? What if they really were valuable paintings and something happened to them as a result of his trying to save them? No. Besides, that would still leave the question of what to do about Spook. Well then, what if he took the boat and stranded Monty and Spooky? No. Monty would know that someone was with Spooky, and it wouldn't take long to figure out who—even for Monty. Then who knows what he might do to Spooky.

Still, there was something in the idea of taking the boat and leaving Monty stranded—alone—with the evidence. "The thing is," Bean said aloud, "how do I get Spookers on the boat without letting Monty aboard?"

Nothing came to him right away, so he decided to follow them. At least he might be able to communicate with Spooky somehow.

It wasn't long before he had the chance. Not fifty yards up the path, he heard Monty's voice coming toward him. There was no time to think. He just reacted.

A gnarled old branch of a massive spruce tree hung across the path, just within reach. Jumping, he grabbed it with both hands and pulled himself up into the thick branches just in time to see Monty and Spooky round the corner, their sneakers slapping loudly against the granite in their steep descent.

"Question is," Monty was saying as he led the way, "what am I gonna do with you?"

"Whaddya mean, 'what're you gonna do?'" said Spooky. "You're gonna take me back to Sands Cove and let me off."

"Maybe," Monty replied slowly. He turned and grinned menacingly at Spooky. "And maybe not." He turned away again and resumed his descent toward the shore.

"What's that s'posed to mean?" said Spooky. "Ow!" The first sentence was directed at Monty. The second resulted from his having been hit in the back of the head with a pine cone.

Monty stopped and looked at Spooky, who was bending over and groping about in the steel blue light of dawn. "What's wrong with you?"

Spooky stood up, holding a spruce cone. "I just got this in the back of the neck."

Monty laughed once and shrugged. "Big deal. Fell outta the tree." He continued walking.

Spooky was suspicious. He stood rubbing the back of his neck and surveying the trees. "Fell awful hard," he said. He was just about to rejoin Monty when another missile grazed his left ear and hurtled off into the darkness. "Hey," he said, turning sharply. "What the—"

"Shh," said Bean from the tree.

"Bean?"

"You comin'?" called Monty from farther down the trail. "We got two more loads to carry."

"I'll be right there," Spooky hollered. "I gotta pee."

"Well, make it quick," Monty called. "You ain't gettin' a free ride without doin' no work."

"You have terrible grammar," Spooky yelled.

"Shuddup," came the reply. "Make it snappy."

"Bean?" said Spooky tentatively. "That you?"

"Who else?" said Bean, dropping to the ground. "I got a plan."

"I'm glad to hear it," said Spooky. "'Cause I think Monty's workin' on one, too. And I don't think I'm gonna like it."

"You gotta get away from him somehow and get down to the boat."

"Why?"

"We're gonna take it and strand him out here."

Even in the semidarkness, Bean could see Spooky's eyes widen. "Are you crazy? Some lobsterman will pick him up, and when he gets his hands on us, we won't be worth the powder to blow us up with."

"Hey," came Monty's call from the shore. "Hurry up."

"Comin'," Spooky cried. "Just hold on a second, will ya?"

"Tomorrow's Sunday," said Bean. "There won't be any lobstermen out. Besides, I think he's gonna have other things to worry about," said Bean slyly.

"Like what?"

"Like the police," said Bean.

"You gonna snitch?" asked Spooky. "He's your own cousin."

"I guess he doesn't care much about the family if he's willin' to risk draggin' our name through the dirt. I don't owe him nothin'."

"Good point," Spooky agreed. "So how do I get to the boat without him?"

Bean thought a second. "Well, he just went on without you, didn't he? Go hide down at the bottom of the path, and when you see him comin' back up, you head on down as if you're gonna get the rest of the canvasses. I'll go down through the trees this way and meet you there. As soon as he's outta sight, we hop in an' haul off."

"Okay," said Spooky, and he started down the path. "But make sure you don't get lost."

Bean wove his way through the thick undergrowth. By the time he arrived at the shore, Spooky was waiting, the painter untied and in his hand. "'Bout time," he said sharply, jumping aboard.

Bean put one foot on the float, the other on the gunwale, and pushed off. He jumped in beside Spooky and turned to the wheel. "Uh-oh," he said.

"What's wrong?"

"Spooky," came Monty's call from up the path. "Where are you?"

"I'm comin', I'm comin'," Spooky bellowed. "Quit buggin' me." Lowering his voice, he repeated to Bean, "What's wrong?"

"He took the stupid key," said Bean. "I can't believe it. Who'd steal his stupid boat way out here?"

"Well," said Spooky as the boat drifted away from the dock in the first, full light of day.

Bean almost laughed at the realization of what he'd just said, but at that moment Monty was thundering down the path, breaking out of the woods to the shore, with canvasses at odd angles overflowing his arms.

"Bean?" he said in bewilderment as he came to a stop on the float. "What're you doin' here? Where are you goin' with my boat?"

The island they were on was really two islands separated by a narrow spit of land. Mostly rocks and mussel shells, the spit was covered at mid-tide and, at the moment, was just barely above water. Unfortunately for the boys, both the incoming tide and the wind were pushing the boat toward the second island. Monty saw this at the same time Bean did. Monty smiled malevolently as he reached in his pocket and produced the keys. "Nowhere is where you're goin'," he said.

He carefully placed the canvasses on the float, trotted up the ramp, and began running along the shore toward the northern island, where his boat was headed.

"Now we're in trouble," Spooky observed.

Bean wasn't about to give up. "There's got to be a spare key around here someplace."

"Where?"

"Who knows? Hidden somewhere. Help me look."

The boys began frantically ransacking the boat.

"What're you doin'?" Monty called as he splashed along the narrow spit of land between the islands. "There ain't no other key. I got the only one right here."

Bean sensed a note of desperation in Monty's voice. "There is another key," Bean said as he ran his hands around the back of the console.

Spooky, who was searching under the stern, looked up. Monty had reached the island and was scrambling to the top of a big rock they were drifting toward. In twenty seconds he'd be able to jump aboard. "It's all over," Monty said.

At the same instant, Spooky's fingers touched a little box in the corner under the stern. "What's this?" he said, removing the plastic box and holding it up for Bean's inspection.

Monty saw it, too. "Hey, put that back. You leave my things alone."

Bean opened the box and removed a key, which he dangled in the air. "Now what do you s'pose this is?"

"That ain't nothin'," Monty bluffed, his face reddening. "That's the key to my truck. You put it back."

Spooky was watching the distance between them disappear as the tide pushed the boat toward shore. "Bean," he said under his breath, "in five seconds he's gonna be able to wade out and grab us. If that's the key, use it."

Already, Monty was stretching to reach the boat. Bean jumped to the helm, inserted the key in the ignition, and turned it. Nothing happened.

"Crank 'er up," cried Spooky. He had taken the boat pole and, leaning over the stern, was trying to push off the bottom with one hand while using his other hand to slap at Monty as he strained toward the boat.

"I'm tryin'," said Bean. "Nothin's happenin'."

"I told you that wasn't the right key," said Monty. "Now, let me aboard before you stave 'er in on these rocks. You get a scratch on 'er, I'll have your hide."

Spooky cast a glance over his shoulder. "She's in gear, Bean. She won't start in gear."

Bean cuffed his forehead with the heel of his hand. "I can't believe I did that." He pulled the lever into neutral and turned the key.

This time the engine roared to life, spraying Monty in the face with exhaust and backwash.

"Drop 'er into gear and let's get outta here," Spooky ordered.

Bean punched the lever into gear and pushed the throttle sharply. The boat responded instantly, and within five seconds they were a hundred yards from shore. Monty, barely audible above the drone of the engine, was yelling and cursing and jumping up and down in impotent fury.

Suddenly Bean pulled back on the throttle and turned toward the island. "What're you doin'?" Spooky demanded.

"I'm gonna get a look at them canvasses," Bean replied. "I'll put up to the float, and you jump out and grab 'em."

Spooky shot a horrified glance at Monty, who, sensing Bean's plan, was already splashing across the spit of land and heading toward the float. "He's comin'," Spooky cried. "We ain't gonna make it."

Bean throttled up a little, and the race was on.

When they reached the float, Bean had to be careful to keep from slamming the boat against the pilings, which would give Monty time to scramble aboard. Meanwhile, Spooky was waiting for the stern to swing close enough to the float so he could jump off and grab the paintings.

"You leave them paintings alone," Monty was threatening. "They ain't yours."

"And I s'pose they're yours, huh?" Bean retorted. He throttled back, slipped the lever into reverse, and throttled up, swinging the stern of the boat toward the float. "Go, Spook."

Spooky jumped onto the float just as Monty's heavy boots landed loudly on the ramp. "You put that down, Spook, or else," Monty threatened, but Spooky didn't plan to wait around to see what "or else" Monty had in mind. He scooped up the canvasses and headed for the boat, but he slipped on a loose piece of pot warp and went down with a thud. Before he could scramble to his feet, Monty had bounded down the ramp and grabbed his foot.

"Let him go!" cried Bean from the boat.

"You bring that boat in here and I just might," Monty replied with a leer.

"Catch!" Spooky yelled at Bean. With a sudden motion that caught Monty by surprise, Spooky tossed one of the paintings across the five or six feet of water to Bean, who caught it between his hands.

"Hey!" said Monty, loosening his hold on Spooky. "Give that back!"

Spooky seized his opportunity. He quickly pulled his leg out of Monty's clutches, sprang to his feet, and hurled himself toward the boat.

"Hey!" said Monty.

Unfortunately, Spooky misjudged the distance to the boat and fell into the water about two feet short of his target. He tried to grab the gunwale to pull himself aboard, but instead he was grabbing handfuls of water and kicking furiously, trying to keep himself afloat. He didn't know how to swim.

"Give me your hand," said Bean, leaning over the side and stretching out his arm as far as possible. Spooky grabbed at it with his left hand just as Monty, who was leaning over from the float, grabbed his right arm, so Spooky was suspended between ship and shore, like a human bridge.

"Saved your life," said Monty with an evil grin. "Now why don't you just come on in here and we'll talk this all over."

Bean started tugging for all he was worth, but Monty wouldn't let go of Spooky's other arm. As a result, the boat was drawing closer and closer to shore. Bean had one last chance.

He seized Spooky's arm with both hands. Then, with an outstretched leg, he spun the steering wheel to starboard and, with a karate-like kick, slammed the throttle sharply ahead.

Monty didn't even have time to let go. Still holding Spooky's arm, he was pulled overboard. It was probably the shock of the cold water that caused him to free his grip on his captive. Sputtering and thrashing, Monty grabbed a trailing line from the float and hauled himself out of the water.

The boat, without a pilot at the helm, was headed at full speed for a shoal of razorlike rocks that stuck out of the water at the head of the cove. Meanwhile, Bean struggled to pull Spooky into the boat.

"Bean," cried Spooky, once he had righted himself on deck. "Look."

It was too late. There was no time to turn. No time to throttle back. Not even time to jump.

19

Things That Go Bump in the Night

AS SOON AS ABBY HAD GOTTEN HOME from the church sing-along, she had gone to bed, much to the amazement of her parents and the Proverbs. Well, she hadn't exactly gone to bed. But she had gone to her room.

After a while her parents came in to say good-night on their way to bed, and the Proverbs and the other guests came upstairs shortly thereafter. Soon everyone was asleep.

Everyone but Abby.

Kneeling beside the window overlooking Frog Hollow, she caught sight of Bean and Spooky as they came up the lane and hid in the bushes. It didn't take a genius to figure out what they were up to.

There was a streetlight in the driveway of the Winthrop House. She was wondering how they would get across the hollow without being seen when Spooky suddenly bolted from the cover of the bushes and disappeared in the shadows on the far side of the street. Ab heard Bean's footsteps below, heading toward the front of the house.

"Now, what are they up to?" she asked herself aloud.

She didn't have to wait long for her answer. Within seconds, the front doorbell began ringing furiously, its shrill cries echoing through the house. Shortly thereafter, she heard Mr. Proverb stomping past her room on his way downstairs, mumbling to himself.

"Diversion," Ab said in admiration. "Way to go, Beaner."

A few moments later she watched as the boys met in the hollow and disappeared through the wood window.

For what seemed a long time afterward, nothing happened.

Twenty minutes or so dragged slowly by. Then a truck drove out of the barn and rumbled down the lane. The truck had only one passenger, whom Ab didn't recognize. She knew one thing, though; it wasn't Bean or Spooky. And that worried her. But the guys might just be waiting for the right time to make their escape.

There was a gentle knocking at her door. "Come in," she said.

"Hey," said her father, opening the door a crack and seeing her kneeling by the window. "I thought you'd be sound asleep."

She shook her head. "Couldn't."

He knelt beside her and stroked her head, the way he always had. It made her feel loved and safe. "Anything wrong?"

"No," said Ab. "Just restless, I guess."

Her father looked out the window. "What's so interesting out there?"

"Oh," she replied, starting a little, "lots of things. The moon. The stars. There are lots of interesting things if you just keep your eyes open."

With difficulty, she was fighting the urge to tell her father what the boys were up to. She wanted him to go with her and find out what had happened. Surely he could stand up to Maud.

But what if the boys were fine? What if they were staked out, watching, or doing something that was getting them close to some answers? She shuddered to think what her father would say if he was looking out the window when the boys came crawling out of the cellar. "I think I'm getting sleepy," she said.

"Good," said her dad, and he helped her gently to her feet. They walked over to her bed, and he tucked her in. "Sure you're okay?"

"Yeah," Abby replied. "I'm fine. Really."

Her dad nodded. "Okay. I was just up and thought I'd come in to close your windows if it was too cold."

"Oh, I'm not cold," Ab replied quickly. "I like the fresh air."

"As you wish, your highness," he replied with a deep bow. She laughed.

"You may return to your room, minion," said Ab, in her royal best. "And do not disturb me again, or your head shall be in peril."

"Forgive me, your misery—I mean, your majesty," her father replied, bowing his way out of the room.

He closed the door and padded respectfully down the hall in his slippers.

Ab jumped out of bed and ran to the window, where she knelt

again on the floor and watched. As the minutes passed, her heart beat faster and faster, and her mind spun with possibilities of all the things that could have happened to the boys. What if they were trapped? What if Mierette had caught them? What if Maud had caught them and tied them up in the secret room? What if the person in the truck had been Maud? What if Maud had knocked the boys on the head with a two-by-four and stuck them in potato sacks, tossed them in the back of the truck, and was driving them out in the woods or down to the shore? What if. . . ?

The longer Ab speculated, the more terrible were the thoughts that came to her mind. After ten minutes she couldn't take it anymore. She had to make sure the boys were okay.

Quickly she dressed and tiptoed down the stairs in the dark. She closed the back door quietly behind her, hid among the bushes, and was surrounded by the cool, quiet island night. The spring popped and sang in the silence. In the remote distance, the foghorn loosed a long, lonely note from atop its crooked old pole on the ledges near Greens Island. Otherwise, everything was perfectly still.

From her place in the bushes, Ab could see that the wood window of the Winthrop House was still open. The big puddle of light from the street lamp presented a problem, but she was pretty sure that no one was awake in the Moses Webster House, and most of the windows of the Winthrop House were dark and shuttered. Besides, this was no time for caution. If the boys were gagged and bound and hanging from the cellar walls by their thumbs, she'd just have to save them.

Had anyone been watching, they'd have seen only a blur as Ab darted across the hollow and wriggled through the wood window, then disappeared into the inky darkness of the cellar.

No sooner had she landed on the musty dirt floor, amid layers of fragrant bark and wood chips, than she realized she had forgotten something important. A flashlight. For a few seconds she stood in the blackness, panting and listening, half expecting to hear muffled cries of agony.

Nothing.

Of course, the tunnel could be soundproof. Or maybe the boys were just being terribly brave.

She decided that the tunnel must be soundproof.

Feeling her way about in the darkness, she soon satisfied herself that there was no way into the tunnel rooms from the cellar. That left one alternative.

Her eyes had grown accustomed to the lack of light, and she could just make out the stairs. She walked gingerly over to them and, stepping from side to side on the treads to avoid making noise, climbed toward the cellar door.

Again, she stopped to listen. When she was sure that the coast was clear, she turned the old porcelain knob, which was loose in her hand, until the latch clicked. The door swung open slowly.

The house was quiet and dark except for two candle bulbs that burned dimly in wall sconces in the hall. She closed the cellar door, took two quick steps to the hidden panel, and in a few breathless seconds was halfway down the stairs to the hidden rooms.

At the bottom of the steps, she again stopped to listen. It was perfectly quiet.

It was also completely dark, without even a dull stream of light through the wood window. Even after one or two minutes, she couldn't see so much as the shadow of her hand in front of her face.

Struggling to remember the layout of the room, she felt her way along the walls trying to find the worn opening that held the secret lever.

First she had to find the right timber. There were more than she remembered, and it wasn't long before she imagined she had been feeling her way up and down the same one over and over again. Finally her fingers detected the worn ledge and the little cubicle. She punched the lever quickly.

She stepped back as the wall groaned slowly aside. It wasn't hard to imagine the immense hydraulic apparatus in the cellars of the Moses Webster House grinding into action. Would anyone there feel the wind in the walls or hear the counterweights rise and fall? She doubted it.

Carefully testing each step with her feet, she descended the shallow flight of stairs and made her way to the tunnel.

"Bean?" she said softly. There was no response. "Bean?" she said, a little louder.

"Spook?" she cried in a desperate whisper. Still, no reply.

Maybe it was worse than she thought.

She remembered a light switch near the door and frantically traced the plaster with her fingertips. Once again the darkness played tricks on her sense of distance, but just as she was about to give up, she found the switch and flipped it on.

A red bulb in the middle of the ceiling bathed the room in soft, eerie light—and revealed instantly that Bean and Spooky were not hanging from the walls or the ceiling and weren't spread out on a rack. In fact, they weren't there at all.

Everything was just as it had been except that most of the paintings and the blank canvasses were gone. The few exceptions lay strewn about the floor. The easels, paints, splotches, and splatters were still there, looking either red or black under the deep red light.

Ab was relieved. All her imaginings were just that—imaginings. If the boys weren't here, they must have gotten out on the other side of the house. Wherever they were, she convinced herself, they were probably all right.

As she pondered what to do next, her gaze fell upon the blank wall at the end of the tunnel studio. What was beneath the white plaster? Granite? Brick? Wood? It wouldn't be hard to find out, if only she could find something to . . . Her eyes swept a small workbench against the north wall. A Swiss army knife.

Kneeling at the base of the wall, she pulled up the screwdriver of the knife and began scraping away at the plaster. At first she didn't make much headway. Layers of enamel paint had made the surface hard and slippery. She pressed harder as she scraped. Eventually she was through the paint, and the plaster began to sift softly down.

"It'll take forever at this rate," she said aloud. In frustration she repeatedly jabbed the screwdriver into the plaster. Suddenly a big chunk fell away. She began chipping with renewed effort, until she had cleared all the plaster from its backing for a space of about two inches. She brushed away the residue with her hand, then bent close to examine the hole.

"Lath," she said excitedly, trying to peer into the darkness between two old, dry strips of wood. Bean was right. If the wall on the Moses Webster side was brick, and this was lath and plaster, there must be a room in between.

All of a sudden, like a wild animal on the trail of its prey, she began jabbing at the hole, first using the blade, then, as the hole grew big enough, reaching in and pulling out large chunks with her hands.

Soon she had stripped away an area big enough to squeeze through. The only obstacle was the lath. She tried pulling at the wood strips, but they didn't give. Then she lay on her back and began kicking at them with all her might.

At first nothing happened, and it seemed that the hidden room was determined to hold onto its secrets. Then, as her muscles were aching after repeated blows, one of the laths snapped loudly. That was just the encouragement she needed. She kicked harder and harder. More snaps followed, then cracks. Then, with a crash, her foot went through the wall.

After a few more kicks, she sprang to her knees and began pushing the broken laths inward and out of the way. The edges that remained were sharp and decreased the size of the hole appreciably, but by this time, in her determination to find out what was in the hidden room, she was indifferent to the threat of physical pain. She made herself as small as possible and began to inch her way through the hole.

"Who's down there?" said a sharp voice behind her. No sooner had the words engraved themselves on the silence than a feeling of nausea swept through her body. As if poked by a pin, she pulled herself through the hole, fear making her oblivious to the cuts and scrapes caused by the jagged strips of wood.

Once in the pitch darkness of the secret room, she spun around and looked out the gaping hole.

"Who's in there?" It was Maud; there was no mistaking that husky, angry voice. She was about halfway down the stairs, Ab figured, preceded by the white beam of a flashlight. She seemed to be approaching slowly, as if unsure whom she might encounter.

A big painting lay on the studio floor near the hole. That gave Abby an idea, and she might have just enough time to pull it off.

Quickly she began scraping up the plaster chunks that had fallen from the wall to the studio floor and tossed them into the darkness beside her. She did the same with the few splinters of wood that had fallen into the studio. Then she swept up as much dust as she could into her hand, and shook it free in the darkness.

"I've called the police," Maud threatened, her voice edged with an indefinable fear. Nevertheless, she was closer, probably inside the second door at the top of the little flight of stairs. Already a trembling light was splashing against the far wall of the studio. Maud was only seconds away.

Ab reached out for the large painting and pulled it toward her, covering the hole at the last instant. She held her breath and waited.

Through the canvas that concealed her, Ab could see the beam of Maud's flashlight racing about the room. Then she heard a low, rattling moan, as if from the throat of someone who was being choked. As Ab listened, the moan grew to a frightening, otherworldly wail, which sent shivers up her spine. The wail turned into a scream, and the scream to a cry. "My paintings! Where are my masterpieces?" The flashlight clattered to the floor, pointing its beam directly at the painting that Ab held over the hole.

"Madam?"

It was Mierette. She sounded sleepy. "Wot eez dee mattair?"

Maud instantly stifled her cry and turned on her maid with fury in her eyes. "How did you get down here?"

"Madam," said Mierette innocently, "I haird you cry. De wall, she was open. I come tru an' see de stairs, an' haird you cry."

"My paintings! My masterpieces,! Maud wailed, in a revival of her agony. "They're gone."

"How eez dees posseebul?" said Mierette, suddenly seeming wide awake. *"C'est tragique."*

"What am I going to do?" Maud shrieked. "I'm ruined."

"Surely not," Mierette consoled. "You mos' go to dee polees. Dey weel fin' dee pantings, no?"

"No," said Maud with a sudden sharpness that stopped her tears. "I can't do that. They'd find . . . No, no. I'm ruined. Ruined."

Once more she shrieked, and the shriek turned to pathetic sobs as she fell to her knees.

Mierette pretended to console her. "Dere, dere, madam. Surely eet eez not so bad as dees. Come opstair. Come. I will make you some tea, no? Eet weel be hokay. You can mak new pantings. Come."

Mierette succeeded in getting Maud to her feet and took her upstairs. Ab could hear her still weeping. The flashlight remained on the floor, pointing blindly at Ab's hiding place.

She waited until the sound of their footsteps disappeared and she heard the door click shut. Slowly and carefully, with the blood pounding in her ears, she moved the painting aside and emerged from the secret room. she crawled quickly to the flashlight, then back through the hole in the wall.

Breathlessly, she turned the strong white beam on a scene that had not been witnessed in nearly a hundred years. Her heart nearly froze in mid-beat as the pool of illumination oozed across the granite floor. Toward the center of the little room, it revealed a tiny pair of shoes, tiny legs, tiny petticoats, and an old-fashioned dress.

Ab clapped her hand over her mouth to stifle a scream as she traced the beam over the little figure. Its full, fat cheeks reflected the light. Its eyes, open wide, stared straight at her and sparkled. "A doll," she said aloud, but the words came out muffled through her tightly clamped fingers. Behind the first doll was another. Beside that, another, and another, and another—a small mountain of them stacked high in the middle of the little room. No two were alike, and each had a unique costume. Some were beautifully simple; others were studded with gems of every description that scooped up the light and tossed it back at her in scintillating shards of color.

Some of the dolls were white, some black, some Oriental, some Indian. Every continent on earth seemed to be represented. Ab gently drew the soft-edged halo of light higher up the slopes of arms, legs, and staring eyes, her amazement growing until she felt she would burst. Then she nearly did.

The summit of the mountain of dolls was crowned with the hollow-eyed head of a human skeleton.

20

By the Skin of Their Teeth

THE BOYS CLOSED THEIR EYES, gritted their teeth, and waited for the crash. But there was none. The boat plowed powerfully on. Bean opened one eye and, looking astern in disbelief, saw the neat, shallow wake cleaving gracefully through a narrow gap in the ledges. He opened the other eye and smiled a big, relieved smile. "We made it."

Spooky slowly opened his eyes. When he was finally able to grasp what had happened, he began to dance around the deck, waving his arms like Scarecrow in the *Wizard of Oz.*

Bean made his way up the sloping deck to the console and pulled back on the throttle. The bow lay down in the water, and the wake washed gently over the stern.

"Wow," said Spooky. "That was some ride."

The sun was fully up as they made their way slowly across the still blue water of the bay.

"Know where we are?" said Spooky.

"Sure," Bean replied. He nodded around him. "We were on Eagle Island. Now we're just about halfway to Stonington. We'll be home in thirty to forty minutes or so."

"What are we gonna do when we get there?"

"Get somethin' to eat," said Bean without hesitation. "I'm starvin'."

"Me, too," said Spooky. "But what about Monty and those canvasses and all that? Are you gonna take 'em to Wruggles?"

"Got to," said Bean. "We've got evidence. There's nothin' else we can do." He stepped aside. "Here, take the wheel," he told Spooky, and he made his way to the back of the boat to retrieve the canvas. "Now, let's see what's so valuable about this thing."

Bean took a gutting knife from a rack, sat on the gunwale with the canvas between his legs, and began to scrape gently at the surface. There was no paint, only a thin undercoat of some kind that was embedded in the fabric. "Well, nothin' was painted over," he said. He flipped the canvas and, with the sharp point of the knife, began popping out the staples that held it in place.

After a little struggle, he had removed three or four staples and was able to peel back the canvas, revealing another canvas beneath. "Aha."

"Aha, what?" said Spooky, his eyes directed intently forward. He wasn't sure whether there was a cage around the propeller on Monty's boat, so he threaded his way carefully through the maze of multicolored pot buoys marking lobster traps scattered throughout the eastern bay.

"There's another canvas behind it," said Bean triumphantly. "And it's got a painting on it."

"You were right," said Spooky, casting a quick glance and a smile over his shoulder. "Now we've got 'em."

Out of curiosity, Bean removed the rest of the staples, pulled away the covering canvas, and held the painting at arm's length.

Spooky saw the reflection of Bean's action in the windshield. "What is it?"

Bean studied the painting. "It's a bridge over a pond," he said. He held it up for Spooky to see.

"Yup," said Spook. "That's what it is."

"I've seen it somewhere before."

"Where?"

Bean shrugged. There *was* something familiar about the picture, but he just couldn't remember where he'd seen it. "I don't know," he said. "Somewhere."

"Is it famous?"

"I dunno," Bean replied unsurely. "I think so."

"Painters sign 'em, don't they? Who's it by?"

Bean searched the canvas carefully. "Mo-net," he said.

"Never heard of Mo-net," said Spooky. "I heard of Michelangelo and Leonardo da Vinci, though. He did that smiley lady, Moanin' Lisa. I never did understand why he called her Moanin' Lisa when she was smilin' like that."

Bean inspected the signature again. "Nope. This guy's Mo-net."

"Oh, well," said Spooky philosophically. "If we had another one to crack open, maybe we'd have better luck."

"I think we'll just turn 'em all over to someone who knows what the heck they're doing," Bean decided. "I don't know nothin' about art. This could be somethin' famous. I know I've seen it before somewhere."

"Just a bridge," said Spooky. "I don't see what's so famous about that. It don't even look strong enough to hold one've them little Japanese cars."

Bean replaced the canvas over the painting to protect it from sea spray, just in case it was famous.

As they entered the mouth of the harbor, Bean took over the helm. He pulled the throttle back to five knots to reduce the wake as they passed boats that were docked along the floats.

The harbor was still, with a few shreds of fog here and there not seeming in any hurry to evaporate. The houses crowding the shore were reflected upside down in the water, and the reflections were shaken into little shimmers by the waves as the boat passed.

Otherwise everything was perfectly quiet.

Too quiet.

"Somethin' ain't right," said Spooky.

Bean eased the graceful boat alongside the public landing while Spooky jumped out and secured the lines. Then they climbed up the ramp to the parking lot.

"Nobody at the restaurant," Bean observed. That was unheard of on a Sunday morning, when lots of people usually had breakfast out before going to church. He took the painting he had just opened and tucked it under his arm.

"Where is everybody?" said Spooky.

"Oh, brother," Bean replied, half to himself. "Not again."

"Not again, what?"

"Nothin'," said Bean. "Let's go down to the fire station."

"Why?" said Spooky as he fell in step behind his friend, who had already started off across the parking lot.

"Just a hunch."

But the fire station, too, was deserted. "So much for that idea," said Bean. "Where could everybody be?"

The streets were deserted. No people. No cars. No trucks. Not even a dog or cat in sight. The town seemed to have surrendered to the seagulls.

"This is spooky," said Spooky. Bean had started up the street. "Where are you goin'?"

"Home," Bean replied over his shoulder. "I've gotta get somethin' to eat." He tried to put a brave face on the situation, but he couldn't help wondering if some alien spacecraft had landed and vaporized everybody. It was a silly notion, of course, but it refused to leave him alone. He wanted to make sure his mother was all right. As he walked along he found himself speeding up, until he was jogging at a fair clip, the canvas slapping back and forth under his arm. Spooky trailed after him.

As they approached the far end of Main Street, Bean heard the low murmur of a crowd of people. "This way," he said, breaking into a run. Spooky was having a hard time keeping up.

Rounding the final corner, they saw a multitude of people mulling around the Winthrop House.

Bean ran breathlessly up to Matty Johnson, who was standing with some other ladies at the fringes of the crowd. "Hi, Matty," he said.

Matty turned toward him and smiled warmly. "Oh, hello, Arthur." She was the only one in town who still called him by his Christian name. "What've you got there? Takin' up painting?"

Bean shook the painting nonchalantly. "No, ma'am. Just holdin' it for somebody else."

"Well, I hope that 'somebody else' isn't Miss Valliers," she said, nodding toward the Winthrop House, where the ambulance had just pulled up.

"Why? What happened?" said Bean, trying to appear as matter-of-fact as possible. There was no doubt in his mind that Maud had discovered her paintings missing and had had a heart attack.

"You don't know? Where've you been?" said Matty incredulously.

"Out in the White Islands," Bean replied honestly.

"Camping?"

Bean deliberated a moment. "Sort of," he answered. "So, what happened?"

"All kinds of things," said Ellen MacKenzie, who turned to them from the group. "Seems that somebody stole all Maud's paintings, though who'd want to steal them, I don't know. Must've been some summer person."

"They did?" said Bean, with a knowing nod at Spooky. "That's awful. Who did it?"

"No one knows," said Ellen. "That ain't one you got there under your arm, is it?" she said with a laugh.

Bean laughed back. So did Spooky.

"Well, thanks," said Bean cheerfully and turned to leave.

"Wait," said Matty, grabbing him by the arm. "You haven't heard but half the news."

Bean stopped. "What do you mean?"

It was Matty's turn to nod knowingly. "They found the Winthrop treasure."

Bean's heart suddenly seemed to be banging against his empty stomach. "They what? Who did? What is it? Where?"

Ellen laughed. "Well, that's what we're all here to find out, ain't it? All we know is it's worth a fortune and it was found in a secret tunnel."

"But you don't know who found it?"

"It's prob'ly gold," Ellen speculated, ignoring Bean's question. Another woman in the group, Charlotte, nodded her agreement.

"Or diamonds," said Matty. Charlotte nodded again.

"But do you know who found it?" Bean repeated, trying to mask his impatience.

"Sure we do," said Matty, stretching out the suspense a little longer. "It was that pretty little summer girl stayin' up to the Moses Webster House. The one I used to see you with all the time."

"Abby Petersen?"

"Sounds right," said Ellen. "Some smart girl, there. Found this little secret room and everything."

Bean's heart was thrashing against his ribs. "So, who does the treasure belong to?"

"Don't know," said Matty. "They're not passin' much information back here. If we could find Leeman Russell, he'd know. I bet he's right up at the front of things. Always is when somethin' like this happens."

"Always is," Charlotte agreed.

"Not that it would make much difference in Maud's case," Matty observed. "I hear she nearly lost her mind over those paintings. I bet it's her they brought that ambulance for."

"Come on," Bean said to Spooky, and they tore off through the crowd.

"He's the one found that tunnel in the first place," said Matty, watching as the boys darted away.

"Is that so?" said Charlotte.

Ellen nodded. "Too bad he was out foolin' around on the islands. He missed all the fun."

The other women agreed that it was too bad.

Spooky and Bean arrived at the front of the crowd just as the ambulance pulled away. They quickly scanned the group and soon spied Abby, standing amid a knot of people who all seemed to be talking to her at once. In the boys' brief glimpse of her, they saw that she was holding a doll.

"I've never seen Abby with a doll," said Bean.

"She's a girl, ain't she?" Spooky observed. "That's what they do."

"Yeah, but—"

"Bean!" Abby screamed. She tore herself away from the clutch of people and ran up to the boys. Right there in front of the whole world, she threw her arms around Bean and gave him a great big wet kiss right on the lips.

Bean felt a blush that started in his toes and worked its way up his legs and his back and his neck and filled his head like a bright red lightbulb. All of a sudden people were crowding around him, and they were smiling and shaking his free hand and telling him he did a great job and asking what it felt like to be rich.

Bean's brain was spinning, trying to make some sense of it all. "Huh?" he said finally, looking at Ab. "Huh?" he repeated, looking at the familiar faces pressing in all around him. Among them were Mr. and Mrs. Petersen and Mr. and Mrs. Proverb, smiling wider than anyone. "Wha. . . ?"

"I told them how we found the tunnel," said Ab. The sparkle in her eyes was nearly blinding poor Bean.

"Huh?" said Bean.

"You did it, boy," said Mr. Proverb, leaning into the little clearing in the center of the circle of people. He held out his hand, which Bean took and shook, though he couldn't imagine why.

"Did I?" said Bean dumbly.

"You sure did," said another voice. This time it was Mrs. Petersen who leaned into the circle. She pinched his cheek, which was okay because it was Ab's mother. "You were right, and we were wrong. Weren't we, Tom?"

Mr. Petersen seemed to hesitate about making such an admission. "Well, I wouldn't exactly say . . . that is . . . of course he—"

"Now just own up, Tom," Mrs. Petersen admonished. "Say it.

Bean and Ab were right, and we were wrong. There was a tunnel right where they said it was. And there was a treasure in the tunnel."

"I think . . . ," Mr. Petersen began, but it was clear he wasn't getting anywhere. Mrs. Petersen helped him.

"He thinks he owes you both an apology." She leaned closer to the kids and lowered her voice. "Now, granted you did some things that were neither smart nor safe, and I hope you learned your lesson." Now the volume went up again, so everybody could hear. "But if we'd listened to you in the first place, we could have done the whole thing by the book. So I guess we can take a share of the blame."

"Treasure?" said Bean weakly, trying to catch up.

"The treasure I found in the secret tunnel," said Abby, holding the doll in his face.

"What're you shakin' that thing at me for?" Bean said indignantly.

"Because this is the treasure," Ab replied with a smile.

"A doll?" said Bean, aghast. "That's the treasure?"

"Not just a doll," said Ab. "Hundreds of dolls, from all over the world. All made of either ivory or porcelain. All in their original costumes. All over a hundred years old."

"That's worth something?" said Bean, a little dejectedly. Like a crow, he had set his sights on shinier things. "Just a bunch've old dolls?"

A number of people in the crowd laughed.

"Tell him, Mr. Carnoby," Ab said to a large man in corduroys and jeans standing nearby. Bean recognized him as an antiques dealer from the mainland who often visited the island.

"I figure the cheapest one will fetch about fifteen thousand dollars," said Mr. Carnoby.

"F-f-fif—?" Bean stammered.

"That's nothing," said Ab with her winningest smile. "Tell him about the queen."

The crowd fell silent as Mr. Carnoby, glad to have an audience, rolled the words around in his mouth. "What she's referring to," he said a little louder than necessary, "is an original Queen Victoria doll, commemorating her jubilee—the fiftieth anniversary of the queen's reign. She's dressed in ermine, pearls, rubies, sapphires, and diamonds, which I estimate will fetch somewhere in the neighborhood of three hundred and fifty thousand dollars at auction in New York." The crowd gasped and mumbled as everyone repeated the figure.

"All told," he continued as the crowd once more became still, "there are two hundred and eighteen dolls. I haven't had a chance to do much more than count 'em, but I imagine the whole collection is worth a few million."

Once again the people gasped and *oohed* and *aahed* and began murmuring among themselves.

"I'd best get back and start cataloging," said Mr. Carnoby with more than a trace of self-importance. With an "excuse me, please" to part the crowd, he made his way back to the Winthrop House.

"They were all on Mr. Proverb's side," Ab resumed excitedly.

"But you'll never guess what else she found!" Mrs. Proverb interjected.

"I think I know," said Bean, with a little shudder. "'Lord, rest my bones as happy here, as she among her babes.'" He turned to Ab. "These dolls are the babes, aren't they? They're what Minerva was importing from all over the world. That means . . ."

Suddenly Ab wasn't smiling anymore. Bean saw her trembling, and he knew she had seen something that haunted her. "Miss Minerva was down there, wasn't she? With all them dolls?"

Abby tried to shrug it off. "Just bones," she said with a faint, brave smile. "A skeleton."

"A skeleton!" breathed Spooky. Abby went up leaps and bounds in his estimation.

"How'd you know that, Bean—that Miss Minerva was down there?" said Mr. Petersen.

Bean turned to him. "Mary Olson's tombstone said so," he replied. Unconsciously, his hand reached for Ab's and found it and squeezed it in sympathy. She squeezed back.

"Who the heck is Mary Olson?" said Spooky.

Bean explained, and as he did, everyone listened intently. When he finished, there was a long, awed silence.

It was finally broken by Leeman Russell, who, as always, had made his way to the front of the crowd, where all the action was. "You know what you guys are?" he said, his voice heavy with admiration. "You're regular detectives. That's what. Yessir."

Several people from the crowd agreed heartily with Leeman's assessment.

Then came one of those awkward times when it seemed as though nobody had anything to say. For a few seconds, people stood staring at the house. Maybe they had the same thoughts as Mrs. Proverb, who was musing what it must have been like for Abby when she pointed the flashlight at the scene in that dark, little room. At first she had seen only the dolls, many of them, dressed in all kinds of costumes whose colors, except for the dust and cobwebs, hadn't faded over the years because of the dryness and total darkness of the room. They had been lovingly assembled in a kind of pyramid; some were standing, some sitting, some resting on others, piled up and up as Abby traced them with her flashlight, until, in an old cane-backed rocking chair in the middle of the mountain of dolls . . .

"Poor ol' Maud's had a bad day," said Leeman, breaking the silence. "First she loses her paintings, then Ab finds the treasure in her tunnel but on the Proverbs' side of the property line."

"Oh, I'll be happy to share anything I come by, fifty-fifty," said Mr. Proverb magnanimously. "That only seems fair, doesn't it? I mean, it's a gift to me, isn't it? So why not pass it along?"

This comment shook Bean out of his stupor. "I don't think Maud's gonna be sharing anything. I found the paintings." He whispered something into Spooky's ear, and Spooky took off through the crowd toward Bean's house.

"You found 'em?" said Constable Wruggles, who had become part of the admiring group. "Where?"

"Out on Eagle Island."

One of the windows of the Winthrop House overlooked the group of people who had gathered around Bean and Ab. The window was open. Nobody noticed when the lace curtain that covered it fell softly into place.

"Eagle Island," said Wruggles. "How'd they get out there?"

"I think I'd like to tell you that a little later, if it's okay," said Bean.

"Well, I guess it'd be all right," Wruggles replied.

"Just give me five minutes. I want to talk to my mom. Have you seen her?"

"Saw her with Uncle Phil this mornin'," said Leeman. "'Bout an hour ago, thereabouts. They was in his truck, headin' outta town."

That's curious, Bean thought. "Which way?"

Leeman shrugged. "Dunno. I just saw 'em go through the street. Coulda turned either way at the other end."

"So," said Wruggles. "You wanna tell me 'bout them pictures? Is that one've 'em?" He nodded at the canvas that Bean held under his arm.

"I got it," said a voice at the edge of the crowd. It was Spooky.

The people made way for him as he waved an old newspaper stained with blue paint. "You was right, 'bag. It's right here."

"What's he talkin' 'bout?" said Wruggles. "What're you talkin' 'bout, Spooky?"

Spooky was almost laughing as he arrived at the bottom of the granite steps leading to the front door of the Winthrop House. He spread out the newspaper and showed it to Bean and Wruggles. On the stained, yellowed page was a photograph of a painting: a painting of a bridge over a little pond.

"So?" said Wruggles.

"This painting was stolen from . . . " Spooky referred to the paper, "a place called the Princep Gallery in Boston four years ago. It's real famous, by a guy named Mo-net."

"You pronounce it Mon-ay, not Mo-net," said Ab. "It's French."

"Whatever," said Spooky. "It was stolen four years ago and never found."

"What's that got to do with the price of rice?" said Wruggles, a little impatiently.

"Show him, Bean," Spooky urged.

Bean held up the frame and removed the outer canvas slowly.

"That don't look like one've Maud's pieces," said Wruggles. "You can tell what it is, see? There's trees, and water, and a duck or somethin', and . . . hey!" His eyes widened as the rest of the painting was revealed.

"This is it," he said finally. "I mean, this is that," he added, pointing back and forth between the canvas and the newspaper article. He took the painting in his hands and stared at it for a few moments, studying the newspaper article, then the signature on the painting, then the painting itself. Finally he held up the painting for the crowd to see. "Well, what do you make of that?"

A collective gasp went up among the crowd, and everyone began pressing in for a closer look.

Wruggles was scratching his head. "I still don't get it," he said.

"I think it's best if we let the kids explain," suggested Mr. Petersen. "Or am I mistaken in thinking you're in on this, too, Abigail?"

"Oh, no," said Ab. "That is—"

"She didn't have anything to do with this part of it, Mr. Petersen," Bean volunteered in Ab's defense. "Honest. When you told us we couldn't"—he wasn't about to say play together; they were too old for that—"spend time together, we didn't. Not except up at the church supper."

"But we were just sure there was a secret part of the tunnel," said Ab excitedly. "And we knew we were just this far away from finding the treasure." She held a thumb and forefinger a half inch apart.

"So I took her place," Spooky explained.

"I didn't get involved again until I thought the boys were in trouble," Ab continued.

"Trouble?" Wruggles interjected. "What kind of trouble?"

"Last night, I was looking out my window up there." All eyes followed as she pointed to her room across the hollow at the Moses Webster House.

For the next twenty minutes, Ab and Bean and Spooky took turns telling their stories and answering questions as their audience, which by this time included just about the whole town, listened with all their ears, so no one would miss a word. This was going to be big news for a long, long time.

"I just knew I'd seen that painting somewhere before," said Bean. "But it wasn't 'til I got here that I remembered the old newspaper."

"So he told me to go get it," said Spooky.

"And all the rest of the paintings are out on the island, you say?" said Wruggles.

"That's right," said Bean.

"And Monty's still out there, too?"

Bean hung his head, embarrassed that his cousin could have brought such shame to the family. He nodded.

Wruggles quickly scanned the crowd. "Amby," he said, pointing at one of the lobstermen in the middle of the throng. "I'm deputizing you to pick three or four other men to go out and bring Monty and those pictures to me. All right?"

Amby agreed, and he picked four men from among those who held up their hands.

"I'd go, but I get wicked seasick," said Wruggles with a wink.

"Monty don't have a gun or anything, does he?" Wruggles added.

Bean shook his head. "Only his .22 caliber rifle, but that's on the boat down at the town wharf."

"Okay, so you boys just bring him in nice and quiet. He shouldn't give you no trouble." As the men made their way through the crowd, Wruggles called after them, "And be careful with those paintings."

He turned back to the group. "Maud's up at the medical center by now. Dr. Paget says she won't be fit to talk to for a while, but I think I'd like to have a word with that maid of hers. Cy, you pick a couple of people and go on in the house and bring 'er out. Might not be easy if there's as many hidin' places in there as Bean says."

Once they had gone, attention turned once again to Bean, Ab, and Spooky.

"What made you think to look under them canvasses, is what I want to know," said Leeman, bursting with curiosity.

Bean smiled. "'Every painting a masterpiece,'" he said. "Maud's slogan. She was right. Every painting was a masterpiece . . . a stolen one. She'd just tack another canvas on top with one of her own paintings on it."

"That's the part that I can't make heads or tails of," said Wruggles. "If Maud stole them paintings, she could've sold 'em on the black market for millions. Instead, she paints her own pictures over 'em and sells 'em for a few thousand to people who didn't even know what they were gettin'."

Bean shook his head. "That's the part I can't figure out, either," said Bean. "Maybe she was just crazy."

Abby had been quietly reading the old newspaper. "I think I know."

"Know what?" said Bean and Constable Wruggles at the same time.

"I think I know why Maud stole the paintings and why she covered them up and sold them." She hesitated.

"Well?" said Bean finally. "Are you gonna tell us?"

"Love," Ab replied, looking Bean full in the face and making him blush.

"Love?" he said. "What do you mean, love?"

"Remember van Gogh?" said Abby. "How he cut off his ear?"

"Sure," Bean replied.

"Who cut off his ear?" said Spooky. This was getting good.

Ab ignored him. "And the guy in New Zealand who ate the car?"

Wruggles shook his head as if he had something caught in his ears. "Guy who ate what?"

"I still don't get the connection," said Bean.

"What did your mother say? 'People will do anything for love.' Right?"

Bean remembered. "Yeah. So? You think Maud covered up the paintings and sold them because she was in love with someone?"

"I sure do."

"Who?"

"CB," said Ab.

"Who's CB?" Wruggles asked.

Abby held out the newspaper clipping and tapped it. "Clifton Bright."

Wruggles read the article and, as he did, a light seemed to dawn in his eyes. "Clifton Bright. CB. Well, those are his initials, all right. But they're Clyde Bickford's, too," he said, referring to one of the town's most respected citizens. "I don't see how that's goin' to get you far in a court of law."

"Keep reading," said Ab, tapping the paper in Wruggles's hand.

"Well, I'll be . . . " he said at last. "It says here that Amelia Williams came up to Camden just after the robbery and that she took the ferry out here."

"Eb Clark says that's when Maud Valliers bought the Winthrop place," said Ab. "Maud Valliers was really Amelia Williams—I'll bet you a nickel. Now, let's just say she stole the paintings. Why? She didn't hold them for ransom or sell them for profit. In fact, she ended up almost giving them away. Why? What would make a person do such a thing?"

"The same thing that would make someone eat a Porsche," said Bean, with dawning realization.

"Here, here, now," Wruggles complained. "Just when I begin to think I'm gettin' a handle on this, you go off talkin' 'bout eatin' Porsches."

Ab explained. "Have you ever read *Ripley's Believe It or Not?*" When she had completed the story, she said, "Love, it makes people do strange things."

"But if Maud was in love with this . . . " Wruggles referred to the paper, "this Clifton Bright fellow, why did she steal the paintings and run away to hide?"

Ab smiled sadly. "Because he didn't love her," she said. "Of course, I'm only guessing, but I think that's the only explanation that makes all the pieces fit. When he didn't love her back, she decided to get revenge by stealing the pictures. You notice there was only one painting left?"

Wruggles studied the paper. "Renoir's *Weeping Widow,*" he read. "That was her."

"Right," said Ab. "That's how Maud felt about herself. It was the only clue she left."

"Not the only one," Bean corrected. "There's also her slogan, 'Every painting a masterpiece.' "

"I guess you're right," said Ab.

"It's almost as if she wanted to be found out," said Wruggles.

"Sure," said Ab. "How else would Clifton Bright ever discover all she'd done just because she loved him."

"Funny thing is," said Leeman, "she goes and gets rich as a painter herself, usin' his initials."

"I'm sure she never imagined that would happen," said Ab.

"Wruggles!" said someone from the top of the steps. It was Cy. "She's gone!"

21

The One Who Got Away

"ARE YOU SURE? Did you check everywhere?" Wruggles challenged.

"Everywhere we could find," Cy replied. "If there's any more secret passages in there, they're still secret to me."

"Well, where could she be?"

"I've got a bad feelin' 'bout this," said Bean, casting a glance at Ab and Spooky. "Come with me."

Before Wruggles could ask what Bean was up to, Bean had run through the crowd, with Spooky and Ab on his heels, and was halfway down the sidewalk to Main Street, with most of the town in tow. "Hey," Wruggles called, puffing after them. "Where are we goin'?"

Less than three minutes later, the kids thundered to a halt at the town dock and stared down at the float. "It's gone," said Bean.

"Gone?" said Spooky.

Sure enough, Monty's boat was missing. A quick scan of the harbor didn't turn it up.

"She's beat 'em to it," said Bean.

"Who has?" said Ab. "What are you talking about?"

By this time, most of the crowd of townspeople had caught up and were gathering around the ramp. Leeman Russell, out of breath but still at the front of the crowd, also wanted to know what was going on.

"I think Mierette heard what I was sayin' up at the house," Bean speculated.

"She did?" said Leeman.

"Must've," Bean replied confidently. "She was prob'ly standin' by a window and, like a fool, I was talkin' nice and loud so everyone could hear. She knew that house. She knew where to hide and how to get in and out without bein' seen. I bet she heard us say that Monty was still out on the island with all the paintings, and that we'd taken his boat and it was still down here."

"You left the keys in it?" said Leeman.

"Of course I left the keys in it," said Bean sharply. "Who's going to steal—"

"I wouldn't go there if I was you," Spooky interrupted.

"No," Bean agreed. "Well, anyway, I bet she heard Wruggles tell Amby and those guys to head out to the island, and she decided to beat 'em to it."

"She could do it, too," said Leeman. "Monty's got the fastest boat in the harbor. If she knows how to drive it, that is."

"Oh, I bet she knows how to drive it," said Bean. "I bet that woman can do just about anything she sets her mind to. She'd have got a good start on everyone else, too, since Monty's boat was right here at the float. Amby and them had to row out to their moorin's to get their boats."

"Well, what now?" said Spooky.

"Coast Guard in Rockland," said Wruggles. "I'll go give 'em a call. Maybe they can get a chopper out there right sharpish."

So saying, Wruggles headed off toward the town office as fast as his legs could carry him. A lot of people followed close behind. Others left by ones and twos to get a start on their day. The excitement was over, at least for now.

Within minutes, Bean, Ab, Spooky, Leeman, the Proverbs, and Abby's parents were the only ones left on the dock.

"Whew," said Mr. Proverb at last.

"Whew," Mrs. Petersen agreed.

That was all anyone could say. It was taking a while for their thoughts to catch up to them.

"Well," said Mrs. Petersen at last, "I guess that just about wraps things up."

True, thought Bean. They'd done all they could do. From here on, it was in the hands of the Coast Guard and the police.

"Not quite," said Mr. Petersen.

"What do you mean, Tom?" Mrs. Proverb asked.

"Well, I can't speak for the rest of you, but I'm pretty sure that Bean and Ab have an apology coming, from me at least." He held out his hand. "Bean?"

Bean took his hand and shook it firmly and solemnly. "I don't know if you need to apologize or not," he said.

"We weren't too smart," said Ab.

"No," Bean agreed. "It's good that everything seems as if it's gonna turn out okay, but we did some things . . . I did anyway . . . that weren't . . that were, well, stupid."

"So did I," Ab volunteered. "I'm sorry, too."

"You're not alone," said Mr. Proverb sheepishly. "I got a pretty good dose of gold fever myself."

"Apologies all around then," said Mrs. Proverb. "Made and accepted?"

"Made and accepted," said Mrs. Petersen.

"Made and accepted," everyone echoed. There were lots of hugs and handshakes, and the air echoed with the sound of thumps on the back.

"So," said Spooky, because he was the only one bold enough to say what everyone was probably thinking. "What're you gonna do with all that money, Mr. Proverb?"

"Well," said Mr. Proverb. "I've been thinking about that while we've been standing here. And, subject to my wife's veto, of course, I think I've got a pretty good plan."

"What's that?" said Abby.

"Well, here it is. You tell me what you think. This town's been awful good to Emily and me. We've got a good house. Make a decent living, and don't have any family to pass things along to anyway." He squeezed his wife's shoulder, and she smiled. "So it's not as if we need the money. We're all right. Besides, I don't think I'd feel too good about taking those dolls away from poor old Minerva, or even moving her, for that matter. She meant that to be her resting place, and it should stay that way."

"Oh, Spencer, you don't mean you're thinking of leaving her there?" said his wife.

"Why not?" he said. "She's been there all along anyway."

"Yes," said his wife, "but we didn't know it."

He hugged her again. "We'll get used to it. No worse than living next to a cemetery. Besides," he said with a grin, "I guess if she hasn't bothered anyone all this time, she's not going to start wandering around now."

"Oh, Spencer," said his wife, but her eyes were merry.

"Nope, this is what I figure: I'll sell a few of the dolls, just enough so I can afford to buy the Winthrop place, and then Em and I will turn the whole kit and caboodle over to the town so they can make it into a museum, tunnel and all."

"Do you think that's a good idea, Mr. Proverb?" said Ab. "I mean, putting poor Minerva on display like that?"

Mrs. Proverb agreed. "I think Ab's right. That wouldn't be fair to her memory, Spencer."

"Oh," said Mr. Proverb. "No . . . I see what you mean. I guess I hadn't thought it out very well."

"How about this?" said Ab. "Leave Minerva where she is, with a few of her dolls, and don't bother her."

"You mean seal up the tunnel again?"

Ab nodded.

"What about the other dolls?" asked Mrs. Petersen. "Sell them?"

"No," said Ab. "I think turning the Winthrop House into a museum is a great idea. Make it the way it was when Minerva lived there. Then put the dolls in the rooms. A lot of people would pay to see them."

"Great idea," said Mrs. Proverb.

"You could call it the Doll House," said Spooky.

"Oh, please," Bean objected. All the talk about dolls was starting to make him uncomfortable.

"That's perfect," said Mrs. Proverb. "The Doll House. I love it."

"So do I," said Mrs. Petersen.

"The Doll House it is, then," said Mr. Proverb.

"I'm goin' to the restaurant and get some breakfast," said Bean. "C'mon, Spook."

"Hey," said Mr. Proverb. "I'm hungry, too. I bet everybody is. Mind some company? My treat."

They all went to eat breakfast, then Ab and Bean and Spook went home to bed, the cheers of the crowd still ringing in their ears.

Late that afternoon, the warm, golden sun slanted through Bean's window and poured all over the room. He awoke to the sound of voices filtering up through the floor register from the kitchen below. Everybody seemed to be talking excitedly all at once. Bean's brain was still tired, but he was able to identify each voice. The first was his mother's. Another was Ab's, then Mr. Proverb's, then Constable Wruggles's. Last of all was a voice he hadn't heard much but sounded most familiar of all. His dad's.

Bean jumped out of bed and ran downstairs and—ignoring everyone else crowded into the kitchen, who had all of a sudden fallen silent—threw himself into his father's outstretched arms. "Beaner," said his father. "How's my boy?"

"Did you hear what happened?" Bean blurted excitedly. "About Maud and the tunnel and the dolls and . . ." He stopped in response to his father's blank gaze.

"What on earth are you talking about, Bean?" said his father with a straight face. He turned to his wife. "You didn't mention anything out of the ordinary, my love."

A quizzical expression spread over Mrs. Carver's face. "Gee, nothing happened that I recall. Seems as if it's been a pretty quiet summer." She turned to Bean. "You must've been dreaming, Beans."

Bean, who was trying to sort things out in his tired brain, looked from one face to the other. "Huh?" he said.

Ab couldn't keep up the charade. Her face widened into a big grin, then she broke into uncontrollable laughter. "I wish you could see your face," she cried.

That's all it took to set everyone else off. Pretty soon even Constable Wruggles was wiping tears from the corners of his eyes.

"What?" said Bean sleepily.

"Of course they told me," said his dad, mussing Bean's hair. "The whole town's talking about nothing else."

"But you didn't hear the latest," said Ab. "You were too busy sleeping."

"What?" said Bean, rubbing his eyes. "What happened?"

"Your dad dropped from a helicopter into a speeding lobster boat, is all," said Mrs. Carver, squeezing her husband's arm.

"You what?"

"Oh, it wasn't really speeding. Just spinning around in circles, really," Bean's dad replied modestly.

"Bean looks as if he's spinning, too," said Mr. Proverb. "Maybe you better back up a bit."

"I'll tell him," said Ab. Everyone nodded. "You remember when Constable Wruggles went off to call the Coast Guard?"

Bean nodded his head yes.

"Well, it happens they had a boat on the way over."

"And your dad was on it," said Mrs. Carver. "That's where I was this morning. I went up to Brown's Head Light, where I knew the boat was landing. I was going to meet your dad and bring him down here to wake you up in the tree house."

"Now wouldn't that have been a waste of time?" said Mr. Proverb with a wink.

"That's right," said Ab. "But while they were on the way, they got a call that a lobster boat was out in the middle of the bay just going 'round and 'round in circles."

Spooky was so anxious to get the story out that he didn't want to give Abby time to breathe. "So the boat your dad was on—the Coast Guard boat—turned around and headed out to stop the lobster boat. But they couldn't get close enough to it."

"So," said Ab, interrupting Spooky with a cold stare, "they could either wait for the boat—"

"Wait a second," said Bean, holding up his hand. "Was this Monty's boat?"

"You got it," said Ab. "Anyway, they could either wait for the boat to run out of gas and hope it didn't hit anything in the meantime, or—"

"Or they could call the Coast Guard and have 'em send out a helicopter," said Spooky. "Which is what they did."

"And," said Ab, "when the helicopter came out, it picked up your dad off the Coast Guard cutter and dropped him right onto Monty's boat."

"Dad!"

"I guess when the captain found out I used to be a navy Seal, he figured that made me the logical choice," said Mr. Carver with a modest tilt of his head.

"We've just got a family full of heroes today," said Bean's mom.

"Aw, shucks," said his dad.

"So, what happened?" asked Bean. "Was Mierette on the boat? Did you find the paintings?"

"No on both counts," said Mr. Carver. "The boat was empty."

"Then what happened to Mierette?"

"Well, that's all guesswork," said Wruggles. "Seems she made it out to Eagle Island all right. We found Monty out there, tied to a tree and lookin' as if he wished he could crawl into a hole."

"And the paintings were gone," Bean ventured. "Am I right?"

"As rain," said Wruggles. "Monty said the last he saw of her, she was in his boat, with the paintings, makin' a beeline for the mainland. Then the boat turns up spinnin' around in circles, and the paintings and Mierette are nowhere to be found. Now that's a mystery to me."

Bean didn't think it was such a mystery. A map of the bay hung on the wall over the old maple sideboard. He stepped over to it. "Look here," he said. Everyone gathered around. He pointed at Eagle Island.

"There are two other islands between Eagle and the mainland. Mierette knew they'd find her in Monty's boat before she got across the bay. So, you know what I think? I think she stopped at one of these other islands, strapped the wheel down with a rope or something—"

"There was a bungee cord attached to the wheel when I got aboard," said Mr. Carver.

"That would be perfect," said Bean. "Give it enough tension to stay fairly straight for a long time before she pitched one way or the other and started circlin'."

"But which island?" said Wruggles.

Bean thought a minute. "Where was the tide when all this was goin' on?"

"About half," said his dad.

"That would mean," said Bean, looking closely at the map, "that she couldn't have got off on Gunpowder Island. She'd've run aground."

"Which means she jumped off at Seven Tree," said Mr. Carver, studying the map over Bean's shoulder. "That would put her about four miles from where we found the boat."

"Well, I'll round up some folks and go out there and pick 'er up," said Wruggles.

"I don't think there'd be much point," said Bean.

"Why not?"

"'Cause all you'd find is where she'd been, not where she is."

"You figure she got off the island? How? Seven Tree's uninhabited."

Bean shrugged. "I don't know. I just think Mierette's too smart to get herself stuck like that."

"Maybe she's just playin' for time," suggested Wruggles.

That was a possibility. "Maybe," said Bean.

"Well, we won't know until we check it out," said Wruggles. "There's still some daylight left."

"The Coast Guard cutter's still here," said Mr. Carver. "They'll take us out. Who wants to come?"

Within two minutes, the Carver house was empty.

It was high tide when the cutter arrived at Seven Tree Island. The search party, which consisted of just about everybody, was ferried to the island in an inflatable craft with an outboard that took them right up onto the beach, where everyone climbed out.

"You go that way," said Wruggles, nodding at the Carvers and pointing to the southern flank of the island. "Petersens, you go that way." He pointed to the north. "And the Proverbs and me will go straight across. We'll join up on the other side. Anybody sees anything, just holler. This island ain't so big we'll ever be out of earshot."

At one time in the past, the island must have boasted only seven trees, hence the name. Now it was thickly forested with gnarled old trees that overhung the water at high tide. They made progress difficult, almost as tedious as the trek across the island through thick juniper and undergrowth. Eventually, however, the searchers met up on the western shore.

"Anything?" said Wruggles, whose party had been waiting when the Carvers and Petersens hove into view almost simultaneously.

The Petersens shook their heads.

"Nothing," said the Carvers.

Constable Wruggles turned to Bean. "Well, too bad, young man. It was a good notion. Maybe we should check out Gunpowder after all. Sunset's still twenty to thirty minutes away."

"That doesn't make sense," said Bean. "She must have come here. I just know she did. Let me think a minute."

"Well, while you're thinking," said Wruggles, "why don't we hoof it on back to the other side of the island? The Proverbs and me beat a pretty good path on our way across."

"Cost us an arm and a leg, you might say," said Mr. Proverb with a feeble smile as he rubbed the scratches on his arms and legs.

"Wait a second," said Bean. "I've just got to think. . . . Ab, what would you do if you were stuck on this island, didn't have a boat, and wanted to get off?"

"Hey, look at the huckleberries," said Spooky, pointing at some bushes just off the beach. He went to investigate.

Ab thought. "I guess I'd try to flag somebody down and hitch a ride. There'd be plenty of sailboats out on a day like this."

"There were," said Mr. Carver. "We saw a couple on our way across in the cutter."

"So, it wouldn't have been that hard for a pretty girl to wave down a boat and get a lift to the mainland, or even over there to Islesboro. That's just a few miles," Bean deduced.

Wruggles picked up the train of thought. "From Islesboro she could take the ferry to the mainland and hop a bus to Portland, or Bangor, or Boston, then to an airport . . ."

"She could be almost halfway to Katmandu by now," Mrs. Proverb observed.

"But," said Wruggles, "there's no clear sign she was ever here."

Bean refused to be swayed. "There has to be," he said adamantly, wracking his brain. At last he had an idea. "What way was the wind blowing today, Dad?"

Mr. Carver thought a minute. "Mostly south southeast."

"That's it," said Bean. "If Mierette brought Monty's boat here, there's only one place she could've put in."

"The cove where we landed, over on the east side," said Wruggles. "So?"

"But," Bean continued, "if the wind was out of the south southeast, any sailboats would have come up between here and Islesboro, on the west side, because they'd have to tack on the other side, and there's no room between the island and the shoals. So—"

"She would have had to carry all those paintings across the island," Mrs. Carver surmised.

"Not necessarily," Bean countered. "Dad said it was about half tide when they found the boat. That means it was even lower when Mierette got here. She could've walked around on the beach."

"Which means her footprints were washed away," said Abby.

Mr. Carver nodded. "No evidence."

Spooky rejoined the group with a big grin on his face. "How 'bout this?" he said, holding up a huckleberry-stained piece of paper, which he handed to Bean. "It's for you."

Bean, with a curious glance, hesitantly took the paper from Spooky. "For me?"

"I found it tacked to a tree up there," said Spooky, nodding toward a little clearing near the huckleberry bushes.

"What does it say?" chimed Mrs. Carver and Abby together.

Bean carefully unfolded the paper and read aloud: " 'My Dear Young Man.' That would be me," he said, smiling at the little knot of humanity clustered around him.

"Bean," said his mother severely, "read the letter or I'll read it for you."

He cleared his throat sheepishly and continued: " 'My Dear Young Man, You were so close, I could almost feel your breath on the back of my neck. Almost. Yours with Respect, Mierette.' "

"No doubt about it," said Mr. Proverb. "She was here."

Constable Wruggles slapped Bean on the back. "Well, Bean, looks as if you got it right again. You ever think about turning your mind to police work, look me up." He smiled.

"Thanks," said Bean. "But it doesn't get us any closer to Mierette. Seems as if this is where the trail ends, as far as we're concerned. As she says," he waved the paper listlessly, "almost."

"Close, but no cigar," said Wruggles.

"You could call the bus companies and see if they've had any passengers matching her description," Mrs. Proverb suggested.

"You won't find her," said Bean as he stood staring west across the bay. The sun was almost setting behind the Camden Hills. A sudden breeze sprang up to wave the orb good-bye. "Not 'til she wants to be found."

Epilogue

Bean and Ab came running up the wood walk with heavy feet. "Don't slam the—" *Slam.* "Door," said Mrs. Carver. She and Mr. Carver had been standing by the stove, talking.

"Guess what?" said Bean.

"Look at the paper," Ab commanded.

"Mierette won a fortune," said Bean.

Mr. and Mrs. Carver tried to focus on the newspaper that the kids were waving in their faces. Mr. Carver finally grabbed it from their hands. "Okay, okay," he said. "Everyone sit down and let us see this."

He sat in the big rocking chair by the window and his wife sat on his lap while the kids huddled around.

"It says she was a private detective," blurted Bean, unable to control himself.

Ab corrected. "A bounty hunter."

"Same thing, ain't it?" said Bean.

"Isn't it," Mrs. Carver said automatically, trying to read.

"It says Maud worked as the assistant director of the Princep Gallery in Boston," said Ab, determined to get her two cents in, "and that she was in love with the director, Clifton Bright."

"That's the 'CB' on all the paintings," Bean reminded everyone.

"It says she loved him, but he didn't . . . didn't . . . what's that word?" Ab seized a corner of the paper and searched through the paragraphs. "'Reciprocate.' He didn't reciprocate."

"That means he didn't love her back," said Bean.

Mrs. Carver lobbed a glance at Bean over her glasses. "Thanks, Bean."

"You're welcome," Bean said with a smile.

"Now, may we read this for ourselves?"

"Sure," said Bean. "Go ahead."

"Yes, go ahead," said Ab. But she couldn't resist adding, "Wait 'til you get to the part where it says why she robs the gallery."

"Who? Maud?" said Mr. Carver.

"That's right," Ab said enthusiastically. "It was just as you said, Mrs. C. People will do anything for love. She stole the paintings to get him back for not loving her. She just left that one . . ."

Mrs. Carver remembered, *"The Weeping Widow."*

"That's right," Ab said again. "It was kind of a hint. But Mr. Bright was *not* bright enough to get the message."

"Neither were the police," said Bean. "It's all right there in the newspaper."

"Is it really?" said Mrs. Carver.

"Yup. Go on and read it," Bean beseeched impatiently.

"It says she covered up all the originals with her own canvasses and paintings," volunteered Ab.

"That's why they were all different shapes and sizes," said Bean. "Because they had to fit over the original ones."

"And then she started selling them," said Ab.

" 'Every one a masterpiece,' " Bean said. "It was another clue."

"Was it?" said Mr. Carver, who had given up trying to read the paper. "What else does it say?"

Bean assumed the narrative. "It says she didn't expect her own art would get so famous. So now she's rich, or will be when she gets out of jail in . . . Hold up the paper, Mom, I can't read it." She held it up. "Five years," he read. "That's a long time. But when she gets out, she'll be rich."

"She sold the Winthrop House to Mr. Proverb, you know," said Abby. "Said she never wanted to come back here again. Said island people are too strange."

"We're too strange?" exclaimed Mr. Carver incredulously. "Talk about the halibut calling the clam seafood."

"The sale comes later, much later," Bean said, rapid fire. "She kept records of everyone she sold one've them paintings—"

"Those," his mother corrected.

"Those paintings to. They've all been contacted, and the original masterpieces have been returned to the Princep Gallery. But all of those people still have a masterpiece, a Maud Valliers original."

"Go figure," said Mrs. Carver with a wry smile.

"And Mierette gets the reward money," Bean announced. "That's what bounty hunters do. They find stuff no one else can find, and get a percentage for a reward."

"Guess how much Mierette got," Ab challenged. "Guess."

"Oh, I don't know," said Mr. Carver. "Fifty thousand dollars?"

"Higher," said Bean.

"Higher? Really?" said Mrs. Carver. "A hundred thousand?"

"Higher," said Ab.

"Higher than a hundred thousand?" Mr. Carver said in disbelief. Suddenly he was sitting up straight. "Two hundred thousand?"

"Seven and a half million dollars," Bean blurted out.

Ab scolded him. "We were going to make them guess," she said.

"I couldn't help it," Bean apologized.

"Seven and a half million dollars?" Mr. Carver repeated. He opened the paper and read. " 'The insurer valued the collection at seventy-five million dollars, of which sum Michelle Cullahany . . . Michelle Cullahany? Who's that?"

"That's Mierette," said Bean, almost laughing. "That was a made-up name. She wasn't even French or Canadian."

"You don't say?" said Mrs. Carver. "She should be on Broadway."

Mr. Carver resumed reading. "Michelle Cullahany . . . here it is: 'of which sum Michelle Cullahany, who single-handedly rescued the paintings from oblivion . . .' Single-handedly with poor Monty's help, they mean," he interjected. " 'Who single-handedly rescued the paintings from oblivion, will receive ten percent from the insurance company and the gallery as a reward.' "

"Ten percent of seventy-five million is seven million five hundred thousand dollars," said Spooky proudly. "We figured it out with a calculator."

"A calculator?" said Mr. Carver. "Why a calculator? All you have to do is move the decimal . . ." The look on their faces showed they were too excited for a math lesson. "Never mind," he said. "I don't imagine Monty's going to see much of it."

"He's already bragging all over town how he helped find the paintings," said Abby. "And how he's going to sue Mierette . . . Michelle, I mean . . . if she doesn't give him his fair share."

"He's lucky no one pressed charges, or he'd be bragging all over jail," Mrs. Carver observed.

"Of course, there wasn't really anyone who could press charges, was there?" said Mr. Carver. "The paintings were already stolen and, whether he knew it or not, he was helping return them to their rightful owners."

Once they told the story, the kids took a few seconds to catch their breath while Bean's mom and dad soaked it all in.

"Well," said Bean at last. "I guess everything's back to normal."

Mrs. Carver sighed. "Gee. It's going to be awfully boring around here for the rest of the summer, isn't it?"

Just then there was a one-man stampede up the wood walkway as Spooky burst through the door.

"Don't slam the—" *Slam.* "Door," said Mrs. Carver.

"Sorry, Mrs. C," said Spooky. "But you'll never guess what just washed up on shore down at Indian Creek."

But that's another story.